Also by Micheal Maxwell

Cole Sage Mysteries
Diamonds and Cole
Cellar of Cole
Helix of Cole
Cole Dust
Cole Shoot
Cole Fire
Heart of Cole
Cole Mine
Soul of Cole
Cole Cuts

Adam Dupree Mysteries
Dupree's Rebirth
Dupree's Reward
Dupree's Resolve

Flynt and Steele Mysteries
(Written with Warren Keith)
Dead Beat
Dead Duck
Dead on Arrival

Copyright © 2020 by Micheal Maxwell

All rights reserved. No part of this book may be reproduced in any form or by any means, electronic or mechanical, including photocopying, recording, or by any information storage and retrieval system, without permission in writing from the publisher.

ISBN: 9798653199820

DUPREE'S REWARD

MICHEAL MAXWELL

Chapter 1

The Quarter Moon Café was at the intersection of Opportunity and Inspiration. It was a kind of unofficial city hall. The mayor and council members would argue, plead, and compromise on the issues affecting White Owl. In election years, a thick black strip of duct tape divided the café in half, Dems on one side, Republicans on the other. The owner forbad, under threat of expulsion until after November tenth, anyone arguing partisan politics. The rest of the time it was a happy gathering of locals and the occasional visitor. Good-humored teasing and strong hot coffee were served up with the best baked goods in the county. The Quarter Moon boasted a long, proud history in White Owl.

In 1927, the Mayflower Bakery opened for the benefit of the Cornish lumbermen who migrated south from British Columbia in hopes of settling on a land offering that failed at the end of World War I. The idea being, the returning Doughboys would jump at the chance of owning a piece of the beautiful highlands country. Few came and fewer stayed. The winters were fierce, rain was frequent, and the roads in and out were nearly impassable half the year.

The Mayflower's claim to fame was the meaty, flaky crusted pasties that Mrs. Bridgette Thompson made up each morning. The lumbermen, sheepmen, and locals would line up and hand over a dime or two and walk away with their lunch or a tasty breakfast. When the morning offerings ran out the bakery produced pies, cakes, and loaves of hearty, brown bread.

The Mayflower was a thriving concern until one morning in May 1933, when Mrs. Thompson was found on the floor of the kitchen, a burning tray of her beloved Lady Finger cookies in the oven, another scattered all around her. The doctor said that her heart simply exploded.

The building sat empty for a year or two until the wife of a local land agent thought she would give the bakery business a go. After all, her children loved her cookies, and friends often comment that they "never had anything like her scones." The truth be told, the children would have been just as happy to have eaten the sugary dough from the bowl, just as much as the over-baked version served up by their mother on Saturday afternoons. The friends, who said they never tasted anything like her scones, didn't mean it in a good way. They often asked if they could take theirs home for later. They were always given another as well. Both only made it as far as the nearest rubbish bin.

Betty's Bunnery, as she named it, only lasted six months. In that time there were only two repeat customers. Betty's husband came once a day to check on her and get a cup of coffee, but his visit often ended in loud tear-filled arguments over why he never asked for any of her baked offerings.

The second was a woman new to White Owl who came for a dozen buns. Betty said she didn't have any at the moment. The woman left bemused but said she would return, and she did a week later. When she requested another dozen buns Betty was forced to admit she didn't know how to make buns.

"Why is it called a 'Bunnery' then?" the woman asked, dumbfounded.

"Bunnery seemed to go well with Betty."

"What about bakery? Since you do have baked goods," the woman suggested.

A flustered Betty admitted that she never thought of that.

That Bunnery closed a week later.

The little building was again abandoned. Over time the windows were knocked out by local hooligans and angry drunks who took their rage out on the poor little bakery with empty ale bottles. A few years later the land agent died and Betty followed her children to Ohio.

In the summer of 1940, Mr. Oswald Ming and his wife May came to White Owl. The clever Mr. Ming went to the county seat and obtained the property, building and all, for the ten years of back taxes owed, two hundred and ten dollars. All summer long the Ming's did repairs and painted. The tables and chairs were replaced with booths. The display cases were replaced by stools and a counter for quick lunch patrons. In the fall the newly converted building opened as a sparkling new, red and gold Chinese restaurant, The New Moon Café.

For twenty years the Mings served up chop suey, egg drop soup, and chicken chow mein to the grateful residents of White Owl who tired of the heavy meat and potato fare that graced their tables at home. On the twentieth anniversary of the opening of The New Moon, Oswald and May announced they would retire. The next day they packed their car and headed for San Francisco. They sold the property for twelve thousand dollars to Peter Twillham, an investor with great hopes for the little town.

The sixties were a time of change for White Owl. The new highway brought curious vacationers in their station wagons and camp trailers. Davis's Grocery became Big D Supermarket. The gas station's two pumps were replaced by a shiny new six pump Flying A franchise. The New Moon was replaced by a succession of hamburger joints, diners, and The Chicken Coop, which served omelets in the morning and fried chicken for lunch and dinner.

State snowplows cleared the highway, and the county bought White Owl snow removal equipment, making the little community accessible year-round. A wealthy member of a positive thinking cult, called Thinking is Creating, built a large meeting hall, and a complex of small cabins for reflection and meditation. The cult held quarterly retreats in White Owl for years, until the leader ran off with the wife of one of the cult's biggest contributors. The faithful tried to press on, but without the charismatic founder, there wasn't enough positive thinking to keep the creativity going. The hall and complex were sold to a big church in Walla Walla and continues to this day as a summer camp and conference center, adding to the local economy several times a year.

    The Chicken Coop closed in 1969. The Seattle holding company that owned the property saw it as just another investment, tax-write off property. The building was leased to a woman who ran a consignment and thrift shop through the seventies and into the eighties. As styles came and went, and the town grew around her, Colleene kept The Clothes Closet going. A department store opened in 1982 and for a time the townspeople thought the second-hand clothes were below their dignity, until the recession in the mid-eighties. The department store closed up. They donated everything left after the big closing sale to The Clothes Closet. Once again, the town folks found recycled clothes fit just fine. The Clothes Closet finally closed in 1988, when Colleene retired.

    There was talk of tearing the building down. The value of the corner lot increased considerably over the years. What was once part of the muddy road in front of The Mayflower Bakery was now a row of paved parking spaces, enlarging the lot.

    Several offers were made. The land, it seemed, was worth far more than the building. One of the serious bids came from ARCO. They intended to tear down the building and build an AM/PM twenty-four-hour gas and convenience store. Unfortunately for them, Gerard Nickerson sat on the city council. His sister and her husband owned the old Flying A gas station, where they ran a small store with gas pumps. The city council refused the permit and the ARCO project was scuttled.

The Seattle holding company was scooped up by investment bankers who invested heavily in ENRON. They filed bankruptcy when their over-extended empire folded with ENRON. The Clothes Closet building was taken over by the town for taxes and though it was listed at a fair price, it sat empty for years, a white and powder blue eyesore.

In the late spring of 1999, Mike Kelly and his best friend, Teddy Auckland, petitioned the city council to hold an outdoor music festival in the meadow north of town. Named on the permit application as the White Owl Summer Solstice Music and Art Festival, no one could have imagined what those seven words would mean to the town and its inhabitants.

Mike and Teddy proved to be a pair of charmingly humble entrepreneurs. The first year, there were around two thousand attendees, twenty-five vendors, and six musical acts that ranged from an acoustic Celtic group, a bluegrass band, Native American dancers, a gospel quartet from Alabama called the Sonshine Boys and a couple of a little past their prime rock and roll bands.

The audience ranged from old retired couples in motor homes to long-haired vagabonds in beat-up old Volvos. The festival was a great success. The whole mood of the town seemed to lift with the influx of new blood, and all the businesses in town saw a mid-summer spike in revenues.

In front of The Clothes Closet, a middle-aged hippie sold large colorful tapestries, Seattle Seahawks blankets, and probably a lot of marijuana. The Sheriff's Department turned a blind eye, not wanting to seem reactionary or unfriendly to all the money coming into town. Apart from a couple of local kids that the giant party proved to just be too much for, resulting in their arrest for a drunken ride through town in the back of a pickup, the weekend proved to be a huge success without incident.

  The next year, Mike and Teddy were welcomed back with open arms. With a larger budget and the rave reviews by vendors and festival-goers alike, the festival grew to a two-day affair. The bill included fifteen acts, most of which were well known in the Americana and Jam Band world.

  The Festival ticket sales topped ten thousand. The venue extended into the side of the Hamilton Mountain basin, which proved to be an amazing natural amphitheater. So many vendors applied that the city offered to close down Main Street and have an open-air market. The promoters were delighted and willingly shared the revenues from the booths fifty/fifty with the city, a move that guaranteed Mayor Chatom's reelection that November.

  That year, four college girls from Portland loaded up a yellow Pinto station wagon with sleeping bags, an army surplus tent, provisions for the weekend adventure, and set out for White Owl. Nancy owned the car and was the mother hen of the group. Halley rode shotgun and played navigator. Misha sat in the back seat and complained. Later, the other three girls would argue over who invited her. Then there was Dara. She was the sparkler on the cake. Just like her name's pronounced, Dare-uh was the first to take a dare, the first one in the pool, talk to a stranger, or approach a handsome young man across the room. She would sing, tell stories, and roll down the window and stick her head out, just to feel the wind in her hair. She drove Misha crazy, but Dara Landry was the glue that held the group together.

The girls seemed to be the essence of the festival, young, outgoing, and very pretty. When the heat of the day got to be too much, they shed their blouses or t-shirts and wore only their bikini tops and shorts. Dara seemed to float through the crowd in her pale-yellow bikini top and flowing, cotton, gypsy skirt. Her long, curly, raven hair bounced behind her and caught the eye of all the young men and some of the older ones. Unaffected, and unaware of her natural beauty, her lovely smile greeted anyone she made eye contact with. A few times she was approached by young men full of themselves and on the prowl for female conquests.

Her friendly but confident whoa, big boy, cool your jets! was never condescending, and left their fragile male egos intact.

When offered drugs or alcohol from a well-meaning partier, her charming 'I'm good' conveyed a happiness in her sobriety that was both non-judgmental and understood.

In the evening, after the last act of the day left the stage, the girls wandered from campfire to campfire enjoying the impromptu jam sessions and sing-alongs. Once or twice Dara's strong, crystal clear, vocal rose above the crowd and they faded away, letting her sing a verse, chorus, or both. She would smile, stand, and curtsy to the applause of the group circled around the fire.

On the second day of the festival, Halley and Dara strolled the outdoor market on Main Street. The crafts, antiques, and variety of food items fascinated Dara, not the items, or offerings themselves, but the way the vendors displayed their wares. The food items were of particular interest to her and she took every opportunity to taste the samples and examine the packaging. The manner in which the cookies, brownies, hummus, and loaves of artisan bread were transferred from vendor to buyer fascinated her.

Long after Halley tired of the booths and returned to the music meadow, Dara chatted and questioned the food vendors about where they were from, how they transported their goods, and what, if any, health and safety regulations they were subject to. Even the most secretive vendor would finally be worn down by the pretty girl with the dazzling smile into giving up the names of their suppliers of bags and banners, and one organic jam alchemist even gave up his secret recipe.

Instead of returning to her friends and the music, Dara walked around town deep in thought. She was so intrigued by the street market she was convinced it was just the kind of life she would love to live. That night, snuggled down in her sleeping bag, she found it hard to sleep. Her mind raced with the images and words of the afternoon's vendors.

On the way home the next day, Dara announced that next year she would have a booth in the street fair.

"What, selling your million and one hair clips?" Misha groaned.

"No, I will bring banana nut bread and chocolate zucchini bread. There was nothing like my zucchini bread, and my banana nut bread is way better than anything anybody had!"

"You don't know anything about selling stuff at a street market. I bet there's a lot to it," Nancy chimed in.

"She can do it!" Halley said, cutting off the objections of her friends. "You should have seen her. She was in her own world. You could almost hear the wheels turning in her head. Those poor people won't know what hit them. I say you go, girl!"

"I do love your nut bread," Nancy confessed.

"And how many loaves will you bring?" Misha asked with a doubtful tone.

"One hundred of each!" Dara declared confidently.

"Right, two hundred loaves of bread! Just how do you intend to do that? Get real." Misha was her usual defeatist self.

"Let me worry about that! I can do this!"

And so she did. The next year she went to the White Owl festival by herself. Nancy and Halley were committed to other obligations; Nancy to her new boyfriend, and Halley to her job at Macy's. Misha, no longer part of the group, wasn't invited.

Undeterred, Dara spent three days nearly around the clock in full zucchini-banana production. Once she fell asleep on the tiny floor of her apartment kitchen waiting for the next batch to bake.

In a moment of total commitment, Dara spent nearly all of her small savings on the six-foot banner that announced Dara's Delights – Homemade Marvels – By the Slice or Loaf! At the last minute, she added …and the Butter's Free!

She draped the banner across her sofa and would stand with a silly grin on her face, just admiring her name in bright red print.

The morning of the big day she was up at four a.m. The banana nut bread was wrapped in commercial plastic wrap and tied with a yellow ribbon. The zucchini bread was tied with bright green. She bought two five-pound tubs of whipped butter, a commercial metal frosting knife, and a thousand six-inch paper plates. If she forgot anything, she thought, she would just make do. As she pulled into the dawn-lit highway, she began to sing at the top of her voice I've Got Confidence, from her favorite movie, The Sound of Music.

As Dara pulled into White Owl an hour later than planned, the streets were teeming with recent arrivals. The traffic came to an abrupt stop right in front of The Clothes Closet. The intersection was the divider for traffic proceeding to the music venues, and the vendor step-up and parking. Though still a couple blocks away, tickets were being checked, and vendor ID badges checked.

Dara took in her surroundings and her excitement grew.

"We're almost there!" she said to no one.

The old building on her left was in rough shape. The sign had fallen down or was removed years before. Multiple layers, and just as many colors, of paint, peeled and flaked, revealing the building's long history.

Dara sighed and said, "Poor old girl, doesn't anybody love you anymore?"

At that moment a cloud passed in front of the sun that sent a slender beam of light exposing the metallic sheen of the words Moon Café. The Ming's old gold paint, for just a brief moment, gleamed like new.

"Nice!" Dara squealed as the cloud rolled by and the traffic moved forward. "Was that for me?"

The Festival didn't officially open until in the morning, but people came early to secure their camping spots and seats in the meadow or amphitheater. At the end of Main Street, Dara flashed her vendor badge with a wide smile and was waved through. A tall gray-haired man with a clipboard and orange vest approached Dara's car window.

"Good afternoon, pretty lady."

"Good afternoon to you, handsome sir!" Dara returned.

"Badge number?"

"1889, Dara Landry."

"Alright, you will be in booth # 26. Nice spot."

"Really?"

"Yep, right at the intersection. Traffic from both streets intermingle. Everybody is going to see your...?"

"Banana Nut Bread and Chocolate Zucchini Bread!" Dara replied. "Come by. The first piece is on me."

"I'll be sure and do that. I'm Carl."

"I'm Dara," she said, sticking her hand through the car window."

"You're up ahead on the right. Numbers on the front of the table. When you finish unloading, you can park in the bank lot behind your booth."

"Thank you, Carl."

Just as she was told, her booth was right on the corner. Dara pulled up and got out and stood for a moment looking at the imposing eight feet of the white plastic table in front of her.

"How am I going to fill that?"

"It's smaller than it looks." A woman's voice came from behind Dara.

"Oh, hi," Dara said, turning. "I thought I was by myself."

"I talk to myself too. The shrink says, 'it's okay so long as I don't answer.'" The woman extended her hand, "I'm Cathy Walker, you already met by better half."

"Carl?"

"Yep, twenty-six years. So what are you selling?"

"Chocolate zucchini and banana nut bread."

"Oh, Rhonda won't like that. Good for you!"

"Who's Rhonda?"

"Preacher's wife. Thinks her banana nut bread is God's gift to the world." Cathy wrinkled her nose. "Too dry for my taste."

"You'll have to come by and try mine. See how it compares." Dara smiled confidently.

"Will do. If you need help with anything let me know. My son Mitch is around here somewhere. He's the fix-it guy. Do you need electricity?"

"No, but I might need some help hanging my banner," Dara said, looking up at the two poles on the ends of the booth.

"Then he's your guy. I'll send him over."

The table was way too big for Dara's needs. She tried to figure out how to display her breads, but even if she put out every loaf, the table would swallow them. The loaves were carefully packed in large plastic tubs. Each layer was supported by sixteen-ounce cups in the corners and one in the middle. The tubs allowed for forty loaves each. The five tubs filled the trunk and back seat of the car. Her banner and sleeping bag rode beside her along with the ice chest full of butter.

The first order of the day was to get the banner up. Dara plopped the plastic roll onto the table and realized that her sign was six feet long, not eight. This is just not what I figured on, she thought. For the first time, her confidence was beginning to show signs of cracking. What have I got myself into? She glared down at the banner she took such great delight in the night before with disgust.

"Are you the one that needs some help?" Off to Dara's left approached a tall, auburn-haired man in an Eagles t-shirt.

"Yeah, I'm feeling a bit overwhelmed at the moment."

"What seems to be the problem?" he frowned.

"I got a six-foot banner and an eight-foot table. If I put everything out I brought, it will look like I'm half sold out, or at worst, have nothing to offer."

"Are you always such a ray of sunshine?"

"What's that supposed to mean?" Dara snapped.

"Nothin', you're just kind of a Debbie Downer. I bet you'd be pretty if you smiled."

"Well, Studly, I'm just not in the mood for your Alpha Male come on."

"Okay," he said softly, embarrassed by his fumble. "What if you just use one table? I'll put one behind you and you can keep part of your inventory there. These poles," he said, grabbing on, "are on stands and I can roll them wherever. What do you think?"

"That would be perfect!" Dara's confidence was on the mend.

Her handsome helper went to work separating the tables. Dara went to the car, suddenly in a panic. Did she forget her table signs? Oh, you've got to be kidding, she scolded herself. She moved her sleeping bag and ice chest, nothing. She crawled into the back seat and looked under the front seats, nothing. After she removed the tubs from the trunk, she scoured the trunk for any of her homemade signs complete with cut out daisies, descriptions, and prices. They were nowhere to be found.

"Is there a stationary store or school supply store in town?"

"Yeah, Olson's just up the block."

"Wonderful!" Dara said, showing her relief.

"They're closed though. Most of the merchants took this weekend off because you guys fill up the street. Most of the stores along here are not what festival-goers are after anyway." There was a slight groan as he pulled over one of the poles. "Whatcha need?"

"Oh, I left my table signs at home."

"That sucks."

"And he's articulate. Never mind."

Within a few minutes, the banner was up and the tables rearranged. "How's that?" he asked.

"Much better. Thank you." Dara paused for a long moment looking at her helper. "I'm sorry if I was a bit nasty with you."

"A bit?" There was a pleasing quality to Dara's helper as he shyly teased.

"Okay, a lot. I apologize. I'm Dara."

"Mitch Walker."

"Yeah, your mom said."

"Alright, I have extension cords to run and panic attacks to talk down. Good luck tomorrow. If you need anything else, my folks are always wandering around somewhere."

"Thank you, Mitch," Dara said coyly. "Sorry again about the..."

"No problem. See you later."

"Come back for some..." Dara spoke to Mitch's back as he turned and made his way up the street. He either didn't hear her or didn't care.

Bright and early the next morning, long before the other vendors, Dara was lugging her tubs from the bank parking lot and to her table. She slept in the back seat of her car and seemed to wake up every time the volunteer night watchman came through shining his flashlight in all the car and truck windows. Still, she was wide awake and excited for the first sale of the day. That sale turned out to be Carl.

"Good morning, I'm here to collect my free slice!" Carl held up a large coffee mug. "Think it'll go good with this?"

"Perfect!" Dara said cheerfully. "Banana nut or chocolate zucchini?"

"Never had chocolate zucchini. Let's go with that!"

"Coming right up!" Dara turned and popped the lid off the tube tagged with a Z. "There you are!" she exclaimed. Sitting on the top of the loaves of zucchini bread were her table signs.

"What'd you find?" Carl queried.

"The perfect start of my day, I found my missing table signs!"

"You made quite an impression on my son Mitch," Carl said, slyly.

"Yeah, Debbie Downer is a hit at every party."

"He called you that?"

"I didn't blame him, I was kind of snarky."

"We have a tough time getting him to even talk to girls, let alone insult them. You are more than just a pretty face."

Dara could feel her face redden as she cut a thick slice of the bread. "Butter?"

"Don't tell my wife." Carl smiled.

Dara handed the piece of zucchini bread to Carl. He looked at it closely.

"This has got real, like garden-grown, green, tubular zucchini in it?"

"The grocery store variety, but, yeah. What do you think?" Dara watched as Carl took a bite and chewed.

"A lot better than the zucchini crap Cathy makes with tomatoes and garlic."

"I'll take that as a compliment," Dara said, hopefully.

"For sure it is! This is great. The gates are about to open. I'll catch you later." Carl turned to walk away. He turned back and said, "Good luck today. And if you see Mitch, be nice!" He laughed and continued down the street.

She didn't see Mitch that day. What she did see were hundreds of people coming by her table and buying her baked goods, fifty cents a slice or three dollars a loaf. The gates opened at eight and by two o'clock there was not a loaf of her bread left. Not knowing quite what to do, Dara sat for nearly a half-hour on the table, feet gently kicking back and forth, and seven hundred and sixty-five dollars in her apron.

She was preparing to leave when a large woman with a bright green, checkered apron approached the table.

"I came to try some of your banana nut bread I've been hearing so much about."

"I'm sorry, I'm all sold out," Dara replied.

"Well, sweetie, this is a big event. Not like a high school bake sale. You need more than a few loaves to get through the weekend."

"I brought two hundred loaves. I didn't know how many to bring, really. Next year I'll plan for more."

"How many?" The woman asked.

"Two hundred, a hundred banana nut and a hundred chocolate zucchini. I was afraid I'd be eating it for months if it didn't sell." Dara laughed. "Do you have a booth too?"

"Yes," the woman said curtly.

"I'm Dara."

"Rhonda."

"Oh, the pastor's wife! Nice to meet you. Sales going good?"

Rhonda whirled around and said, "Maybe they will be now." And off she went down the street.

It took a bit of doing, but Dara was able to pull over the poles and untie her banner. She hummed I've Got Confidence as she carefully rolled up the banner. "Dara's Delights, indeed!" she said, as she put the banner under her arm, picked up the stack of empty tubs, and headed for her car.

As she rounded the corner of the bank, a voice called out, "Where you goin'?" It was Cathy, walking quickly towards her.

"Oh, hello! All sold out! What a great day!"

"Will you be back next year?"

"For sure! Put me on the list. Want me to pay now?"

"No, no we'll send you the application next spring. I'm so happy you did well. I saw Rhonda stomping off from your booth." Cathy laughed. "She hasn't sold diddly. I love it!"

"Oh, come on," Dara said, frowning.

"No, she's madder than a boiled owl. She's been just sitting down there. Even the locals are talking about your stuff. Carl was nuts about your chocolate zucchini bread. I meant to get over and get a loaf."

"Next year I'll bring you a loaf. I just love this town!"

"It seems to have taken a shine to you, too! Especially, Mitch. What did you say to the kid? He's like a different person."

"Nothing, really, honest, nothing. He was so sweet. I was kind of snotty to him. Please tell him how sorry I am, I was out of line."

"No problem. Have you got somebody? Boyfriend, or…? Oh, gee, that's tacky. Forget I asked. It's a mother thing."

"Nope, free as a bird and open to possibilities." Dara smiled, knowing she wouldn't be back for a year. Anything could happen in a year.

"Here, let me give you a hand." Cathy took the tubs and walked Dara to her car.

On the way out of town, she smiled as she passed the Moon Café. "See ya later!"

Dara was a vendor for the next two years. Mitch was waiting for her the next year and they got along much better. She brought six hundred loaves, two hundred each of the banana nut and chocolate zucchini, and two hundred of a new addition, chocolate chip banana. By noon the second day, all six hundred were sold.

To celebrate, she accepted an invitation to dinner with Mitch. Dara ended up staying at Cathy and Carl's an extra day. Mitch showed her the town, told of his plans to become a fireman and how, in the winter, he drove the snowplow. Dara found the bashful, small-town hunk quite charming, and when she left they exchanged numbers and promised to stay in touch. In a moment of abandon, Dara gave Mitch a big kiss on the cheek.

In the months that followed, they chatted, emailed, and texted each other often. In December she came the day after Christmas and rode shotgun in the snowplow, and gave Mitch their first real kiss. As much as Dara hated to admit it, she was falling for Mitch, his family, and the little town.

Dara came three times to visit White Owl that year. Work kept her from visiting more. On Valentine's Day, she received a dozen roses and a simple note from Mitch that said. "You're the one!"

Dara confided in Halley at lunch one day that she was in love with her firefighter boyfriend. "I think we just might end up married! Can you believe it? He hasn't asked or anything, but come spring, don't be surprised."

Dara married Mitch in June of that year. Rhonda's husband officiated and the whole town seemed to turn out. Halley was maid of honor, Nancy was her bridesmaid. Mitch asked his lifelong friend, Ryan, to be his best man, and a very handsome fellow fireman was his groomsman.

Halley and the groomsman dated on and off for a few months but the distance was too big an issue.

Dara loved her new in-laws. Her parents divorced when she was little and she never heard from her father again. During Dara's third year of high school, her mother remarried. Their relationship was permanently damaged. She hadn't spoken to her mother in several years and received no RSVP for her wedding invitation.

The newlyweds settled into a two-bedroom A-Frame just outside of town. Dara became a perfect housewife and worked part-time at Olson's Stationery.

Shortly after their third anniversary, Mitch went with a group from Washington to fight California forest fires. The money was really good, and they planned to put the extra away to start a family the following year.

Dara's Delights made their sixth appearance at the Music Festival street fair. As always, her baked goods were a huge hit. The line expanded to six items. She arranged through a friend to use the kitchen at the elementary school to produce her biggest inventory ever. She recruited Halley to help her work the booth, now expanded to the full eight feet.

Dara was loved by the town's people, and Carl and Cathy insisted she stay a couple of nights a week while Mitch was away. She began to think seriously about having a baby. Mitch made good money, and they were looking into buying a bigger house. She was happier than at any time in her life.

Dara smiled and waved as she saw her mother and father-in-law coming up the street toward her booth. She was giving a customer their change when the pair stepped up to the booth.

Dara's stomach jerked hard when she looked up into Cathy's red-eyed, tear-stained face. She looked quickly to Carl. He was pale and seemed to be struggling to breathe.

"What's wrong?" Dara asked.

"It is Mitch, sweetie. He's been killed," Carl said.

Dara heard nothing after that. She vaguely remembered Halley taking her in her arms, feeling her hot cheek, and the sound of her sobbing.

There were no remains to be returned to White Owl. A flag-covered casket sat at the front of the church where they took their vows. Mitch's White Owl Fire Department helmet sat atop the casket, but Dara knew the wooden box was empty. She refused to go to Carl and Cathy's after the funeral. She didn't want to hear anyone say how sorry they were, what a great guy Mitch was, or if there was anything they could do, just ask. She went home alone. Dara laid in their bed and listened to Mitch's favorite Eagles album over and over.

In the days to come, she considered going back to Portland, but the idea was soon dismissed, White Owl was now her home.

Chapter Two

The Greyhound Bus Lines didn't have a station in White Owl. Passengers boarded and exited right in front of the Post Office, mostly because there was a good place for the bus to turn around at the end of the street.

Dupree's back ached from sitting up all night. His seat partner was still sleeping it off when he stood to leave the bus. Pack in hand, he stepped into the morning air with a grunt. He stretched, twisted, and took a deep breath of the amazingly crisp air.

He walked half a block before he stopped to take a real look around. The little town was clean; the mountains that surrounded it were snowcapped even this late in the year, and the buildings and businesses looked like they dropped right out of an old movie. Many doors and some windows announced the names and hours of the businesses in gold gilt paint. Hawke's Pharmacy was the most elaborately painted, with its name spelled out in a beautiful, early twentieth-century script.

There weren't many cars on the streets, and the bus sounded like thunder as it roared past Dupree and back to the highway. The other two passengers that got out in White Owl were greeted by a man in a heavy four-door pickup.

"Well, here you are," Dupree said to himself, realizing the town wouldn't come awake for another couple of hours.

Somehow, White Owl was not what Dupree was expecting. The image of artists, hippies, and craftsmen, with shops lining the street, didn't square with what he saw before him. It was certainly more Mayberry than Woodstock.

Dupree was overcome by a feeling he couldn't quite identify. It wasn't disappointment exactly, but it wasn't excitement either. His early morning arrival perhaps wasn't the best time to size up the community. He traveled so many miles with an image of his own creation floating around in his head that the reality was hard to process. It's a bit like having Ringling Brothers Circus imagined and arriving at a two goat, traveling petting zoo.

Then Dupree stopped walking and chuckled aloud. "Who cares? You had no direction but north when you left L.A. Just because some kid gives you the name of a town doesn't mean you are somehow required to stay there."

Dupree put his hand out in front of him and stuck his thumb up. Still works, he thought. He shrugged and kept walking toward Inspiration Street. He vaguely remembered passing a coffee shop on the bus. That might be a way to get a better idea of where he landed.

The eight spots in front of The Quarter Moon Café were all filled. That's a good sign, he thought, as he walked across the street.

"You could be arrested for jaywalking you know!" a white-haired man called from where he was getting in his car. "But not here!" He burst into laughter at his joke and got in the car.

Dupree returned the wave as the man pulled by. The café's hours of operation were painted in white at the bottom of the café's front door. Dangling from a gold cord a neatly printed sign read, Stomp your feet before you come in! Leave your mud and dirty talk outside! – Dara.

Dupree tried to imagine a similar sign in L.A. It wouldn't be ten minutes before somebody sued Dara for infringement of their freedom of speech. Must be like jaywalking, he thought, but not here.

The sound of loud talk and laughter greeted Dupree when he opened the door. He felt like a guest arriving late to a party. There was a seat at the counter, but he didn't like counters much. Near the corner was a booth a boy of about sixteen was clearing. Dupree headed for that one.

"If you did, nobody would probably notice!" a man called from across the room, and the café exploded in laughter.

"Just 'cause you're too cheap to close and go on vacation, doesn't mean it's a bad idea," a man in a grimy baseball cap returned.

"You never closed before," another man called out. "Why now?"

"I bet Frank's got him a beautiful Asian mail order bride off the Internet!"

"Or Russian!"

The whoops and pounding of tabletops were deafening in the confined space. The boy with the bus tray rolled his eyes as he passed Dupree. A ringing bell cut through the clanging of dishes and silverware. The room was almost instantly quiet.

"I hope she's blind. Otherwise, it will never work out!" a man said a little above normal table talk.

"Tim!" A woman's voice reprimanded the man like an errant child.

Dupree glanced around but saw only men. The exception was the wide-hipped woman in a blue plaid apron approaching his booth. He was looking right at her and the voice didn't come from her.

"Good morning, chili cheese egg puff, fried potatoes, and fruit or a slice of caramel banana bread is the special of the day. Coffee?" She didn't wait for a reply. In what seemed one movement, she flipped the cup in front of Dupree and filled it. "Here's your menu, back in a minute." Before Dupree could respond, she was gone.

The menu was a simple affair, two sheets of paper encased in a plastic folder. On the front was a montage of pictures of the building in old black and white photos. Overlaid, much larger and in color, was a present-day picture of the café. Under the photo was a simple line of text, "A Little Building Making People Happy Since 1927."

The first page of the menu was divided into two sections, breakfast and lunch. The bill of fare was simple, breakfast: Egg, house-made sausage, bacon, potatoes, toast, pancakes, and coffee or orange juice.

The only question was in what quantity; the prices varied accordingly.

Lunch was even simpler: Hamburgers, single or double, cheese or not, bun or Dara's whole wheat bread. Two sandwiches were offered, turkey and roast beef. There were daily specials ranging from meatloaf, tuna casserole, the El Jefe burrito, chicken pot pie to chicken and dumplings. No special on Saturday and The Quarter Moon was closed on Sunday.

The right side was an assortment of baked goods, by the slice, or the loaf, pie or cake. The loaf cakes came with butter or cream cheese, the cakes and pies with or without a scoop of vanilla ice cream or, in the case of the apple pie, a slice of melted cheddar cheese. Dupree thought what a great concept, offer just a few items, do it well, and only be open until two o'clock.

"So, what'll it be?"

Dupree looked up at the waitress who smiled but didn't mean it. "It looks pretty simple."

"You just gotta choose."

Taking a quick glance up again, Dupree read the waitress's name tag, TJ. "Teresa Janette?"

"Tammy Jo."

"Dupree."

"That's not on the menu," she said with a shake of her head.

"Not feelin' it this morning?"

"The natives are restless."

"I heard the bell. Is that the noise alarm?" Dupree asked.

"That's Dara's way of saying 'shut the hell up.' These guys get so wound up sometimes I go home with my ears ringing."

"I think I'll try the chocolate zucchini bread with cream cheese."

"One slice or two?"

"I'll start with one. Who knows, I may want to try another kind."

TJ was gone without comment. Dupree looked around the small café. The decorations were simple but with a crisp modern look. Not the kind of thing you would expect from a place that only holds about thirty customers, in an equally small mountain town.

A man and a woman came in the front door and looked around for a seat. Spotting Dupree, they started toward the corner booth.

"Mind if we join you?" the man asked, reaching the table.

"Doesn't matter, we're going to anyway," the woman chimed in.

Dupree chuckled and said, "Then that appears to be settled. Have a seat."

The couple slid in across from Dupree and got comfortable.

"This place is kind of informal. Most of the guys just sit wherever," the man said.

"I'm Cathy. This is Carl. Our daughter-in-law owns the place."

"It seems to be one of a kind. I like the atmosphere, especially the bell."

"Nice touch, huh? I'm not too sure about it sometimes," Carl grinned.

"I'm Dupree, by the way. I was in an accident," Dupree lied, catching Cathy staring at his black eyes.

"Looks like it hurt," Carl said.

"Not as bad as when it got popped back." Dupree smiled.

"What brings you White Owl?" Cathy asked.

"No filter." Carl shrugged.

"Not needed. No secrets." Dupree took a sip of coffee. "I'm looking for a home."

"Ray Perlang is a good honest Real Estate guy."

"Little early for that. I just got here about fifteen minutes ago."

"Why White Owl?" Cathy questioned.

"Believe it or not, a kid on a bus bench in Stockton, California recommended it. It isn't quite what he described, but..."

"He was probably here for the Festival. Total make-over for the Summer Solstice," Carl offered.

"Here you go." The waitress set a plate in front of Dupree with four slices of different breads and a large scoop of cream cheese.

"But I..."

The waitress was gone in the blink of an eye.

"You only ordered chocolate zucchini, right?" Cathy asked.

"How'd you know?"

"It's a tradition. If you order the chocolate zucchini, boss's orders you automatically get banana nut, chocolate chip banana, and caramel banana to go with it. No charge of course."

"Like picking the right lottery number?" Dupree smiled, obviously confused.

"Not quite as fun," Carl said.

"Dara was married to our son Mitch. You never saw two people so much in love. She came to town for the festival, and the next year came back with her baked goods for the street market. The first thing Mitch ever tasted of hers was chocolate zucchini bread."

"Mine too," Carl interjected.

Cathy smiled sweetly. "They really hit it off and before you know it, they were married. Mitch went to California to fight forest fires down by L.A. In the freak shift of wind, he was caught in the center of the blaze. We lost our son, and Dara lost her heart."

"I am so very sorry," Dupree said softly.

"So, in his honor, anytime someone orders chocolate zucchini they get the four kinds she was serving when they got married." Carl smiled sadly.

"She must be a lovely person," Dupree said.

"She used the insurance money to buy this old building. Started out just serving baked goods and coffee, then little by little it turned into what you see today."

"She makes a good living and to our everlasting delight, it kept her with us. She is truly our daughter now. We love her as much as any child we could have ever had," Cathy said, with emotion welling.

"She can't replace our Mitch, of course, but she sure has helped ease the pain of our loss." Carl reached over and patted his wife's hand.

Cathy sat up a bit straighter and cleared her throat. "So, tell us about you. What's your story there, Black Eye Susan?"

"For starters, I lied. For which I ask forgiveness. It was easier than explaining what really happened to my nose. I was hitchhiking and was robbed by the driver. He slammed me across the face with a gun and kicked me out of the car."

"You know I have to ask," Cathy said, cocking her head to one side. "You don't look like the hitchhiking type."

"Too long a story for today." Dupree looked down at the plate and tore off a piece of bread. "It is kind of why I'm sitting here today. If I stick around, I promise to give you the whole story right here at the café and pick up the check."

"Tell me one thing," Cathy said, staring Dupree straight in the eyes. "You ever served time?"

"Cathy!" Carl scolded. "Honest to God, sometimes. Sorry, like I said, no filter."

"I got my reasons," Cathy shot back.

"Stop before the bell rings again," Dupree kidded. "No. Never been arrested, never been convicted, and never served time."

"Happy?" Carl chided.

"Yes, as a matter of fact." Cathy gave Dupree a big smile.

"Tell me," Dupree said, anxiously trying to change the subject, "is there a good hotel in town?"

"Good would be stretching it, but The Hodder is all we really have in town. There's a Super 8 Motel about five miles back down the highway."

"You need to be at Grammy Morrow's Guest House. She takes on long and short term boarders. I can call her for you if you'd like. Clean, quiet, and she includes dinner. Her pork roast is worth the price of rent. Oh, you're not Jewish, are you?"

"No, Muslim," Dupree said, very straight-faced.

"Really?" Cathy said sharply.

"No. Would it matter?"

Cathy was still holding her breath, not sure how to respond.

"I was joking. I'm not Jewish, but Muslims don't eat pork either, get it?" Dupree felt foolish. A good example of why he tried not to be funny.

"I can call Grammy if you want. She likes people who come with a good reference."

"And I still get a good reference?"

"I got a good feeling about you, Mr. Dupree. I think..."

"Filter," Carl interrupted.

"Just Dupree. And yes, I would appreciate an introduction."

"Anything else?" the waitress asked Dupree, setting down a piece of apple pie and a glass of milk in front of Carl.

"No, that was great."

"A buck for the coffee. I'll get you up front when you're ready."

"Cheese melted enough Carl."

"Perfect as always, Tammy."

"Carl, you know she doesn't like that," Cathy scolded.

"I know, that's why I do it." Carl chuckled.

"You can follow me over to Grammy's while Carl works on his pie."

"That would be great. If Carl doesn't mind."

"In case you haven't noticed, what I mind, or don't mind, has little relevance around here. She's gonna do it anyway."

"Where are you parked?" Cathy asked.

"Right here."

"What do you mean?" Cathy frowned.

"I came in on the bus. No car, just me."

"Where's your bags?"

Dupree lifted his pack and grinned. "This is it."

"Well, you certainly travel light," Carl said, taking a bite of pie.

"Then I guess I'll be giving you a ride then. You ready?"

"I guess so." Dupree slid out of the booth and stood. He reached in his pocket and pulled out a five-dollar bill.

"I got this," Carl said. "Welcome to White Owl."

"I'll introduce you to Dara on the way out."

Cathy greeted and teased half a dozen people on her way to the counter.

"Hi Chris, Dara in the back?"

"No, she ran to the bank."

"Darn, I wanted her to meet my new friend Dupree."

"Another one Cathy? Really?" The cashier said, shaking her head.

"Oh, hush." Cathy turned and headed for the door, with Dupree dutifully following along behind.

The ride to the boarding house was filled with more explanations and commentary on the town and its inhabitants. With a little updating the Beaver

Cleaver, Donna Reed, and the Father Knows Best gangs could fit right in. The boarding house was only a few blocks from The Quarter Moon, but Cathy insisted on a few detours to show Dupree the bank where Carl was manager, the Post Office, Big D Supermarket, City Hall, and Barker's Supply, just in case he needed a few more clothes. If Cathy was anything, she was subtle.

The woman that opened the door at Morrow's Guest House was old, gray, and bent. A quarter of her weight must have been her massive bosom. She was dressed in a navy-blue rayon dress and a string of white pearls. Her ankles poured over the sides of her lace-up black shoes. She reminded Dupree of the old lady's picture in the See's Candy Store, with her little rimless glasses.

"Hi, Grammy! This is Dupree. He needs a place to stay while he checks out White Owl. I said you need look no further than Grammy Morrow's."

"Hello there, come on in." The old lady's eyes twinkled with a youthful enthusiasm.

"Good morning," Dupree said, as he stepped inside.

"I'll leave you two to it. I'll see you around!" Cathy kissed the old woman on the cheek, gave Dupree a big smile, and left the house.

"How long will you be wanting to stay?"

"Shall we say two weeks to start?" he suggested, almost as an apology.

"That will be two hundred dollars. You can pay me when you can."

Dupree nodded and opened his pack and pulled out four hundred dollars. "Now will be fine," he said, handing Grammy fourteen hundred dollars.

"Oh, sugar, this is way too much!" She handed Dupree back all but two hundred dollars. "I meant for the two weeks."

Dupree was speechless; two hundred dollars was less than he ever paid for a night in a hotel. He couldn't imagine paying that much for two weeks. He slipped the bills into his front pocket and suddenly wondered what he'd gotten himself into.

"Well, let's get you settled. Better get your bags." Grammy looked at the front door.

"This is it." Dupree shrugged.

"Oh, dear. Well, alright." Grammy started up the stairs.

At the top of the stairs were three doors. "Mr. Cooper is in the room at the end of the hall, Mr. Perez is next door, and we'll put you here." She reached over and opened the door. "I call this the cowboy room. I hope it is okay."

The room was decorated with heavy oak furniture. The bed was wide and covered with a thick comforter. A massive dresser sat in the corner of the room. It and the nightstand had thick marble tops. On one wall was an original poster from Buffalo Bill's Wild West Show and on the other a large Remington print of Custer's Last Stand.

"This is incredible!" Dupree said as if seeing a comet for the first time.

"Oh, I am so glad you like it. My late husband Russell just loved this furniture and would never let me get rid of it. The pictures used to hang in his office. He was a surveyor."

"He had great taste in women and décor," Dupree grinned.

"Flirt!" Grammy slapped Dupree on the arm. "Bathroom's at the right, across the hall."

"Great."

"A few house rules. There are just three. No women in the room. No smoking. No drinking or drugs, I won't abide it. I am a God-fearing woman and won't stand for any foolishness."

"There shouldn't be any problems there. Don't smoke, don't drink, drugs are illegal, and I don't do well with women."

"I don't believe that for a minute. Even with those black eyes, I can see you're a handsome brute."

"I'm serious. I've given up drinking, never smoked or tried drugs."

"I'm going to have my hands full with you, I can tell." The old lady giggled with a girlish smile. "Dinner is included in the rent and is served exactly at six. If you're not here by ten after you have to fend for yourself."

"Sounds fair." Dupree looked around the room again and smiled. "What is that?" He pointed at a rusted metal object hanging above the closet door.

"Beaver trap! Mess with it at your peril."

Dupree could tell she wasn't kidding.

"How shall I address you?" Dupree asked.

"Everybody in town calls me Grammy, so until we are engaged I guess you can, too." The old lady winked at Dupree and turned for the stairs.

"Thank you so much for taking me in," Dupree said to her back.

Grammy just waved her hand. Dupree went back into the room and closed the door. He kicked off his shoes and walked to the bed. He pushed down on the mattress with both hands and nodded.

"Perfect."

He crossed the room and put his pack on the dresser. He opened it and took out his underwear, socks, and shirts. Pulling out the top dresser drawer, he laid them gently next to the black leather-covered Bible. It didn't say Gideon's on the cover so he figured it belonged to Grammy.

Reaching deep into the pack, he pulled out his envelope of money and added up his expenses. A hundred used for his first meal and car-motel in Bakersfield. I-hop, ice cream, bus fare, then Cutter got the rest. Two hundred to Grammy. He should have forty-seven hundred left.

He looked over every inch of the room. Finally, he pulled open the dresser drawer again, slipped the envelope into the back of the Bible, and shoved the drawer closed. Moments later, he slipped out his door to the bathroom across the hall. It was just as he expected, subway tiles on the walls, a claw foot tub with a shower head installed on the wall above. The toilet must have been a hundred years old. The tank was above Dupree's head and was fitted with a long brass chain with a wooden handle for a flusher. He did his business, washed his hands, and slipped back across the hall.

Exhausted from the all-night bus ride and his alcoholic seatmate, Dupree stretched out on the bed and closed his eyes. Within minutes he was fast asleep. The bed was as soft and comforting as a mother's hug, and as warm as a May afternoon. Dupree slept for nearly three hours and didn't roll over. He woke rested and a bit surprised at his surroundings.

He went downstairs and found Grammy in the front room in a rocking chair, knitting by the window.

"If a person were looking for work in a town like White Owl, what kind of skills would they need to possess?" Dupree asked, entering the living room.

"They're always hiring loggers. The plywood mill in Barkley might be hiring. What kind of work do you do?"

"Well, it has been a while since I did manual labor. I worked in a shoe store sometimes as a kid to help out my dad. Since college, I have done office work, mostly." Dupree felt a bit foolish, not answering her question directly.

"Hmmm. Well, I'm at a bit of a loss then. You might ask around The Quarter Moon, most everyone who might know something in town passes through there if not daily, then at least once a week. It is the unofficial City Hall, you know."

"It was quite a place alright."

"Dara might know somebody. She hears all the news of the town first. I'm sorry I can't be more helpful, years past I was part of the tella system hereabouts, but now I'm too old to get out much, and most of my friends have died."

"Tella system?" Dupree questioned.

"Where are you from? Telephone, Telegraph, Tella woman!" Grammy rocked in her chair and let out a bigger laugh than even she expected.

"That's a good one," Dupree said. "I'll have to remember it."

"I'm going to take a walk. See you for dinner."

"Have fun," Grammy said, not looking up.

The boarding house was just a couple of blocks from the main downtown area, all three blocks of it. Dupree walked up one side of the street and down the other. People passed and said good morning, and merchants nodded as he passed their establishments. There were no help wanted signs and most of the businesses were very small and looked like owner-operated concerns.

In the middle of the block in front of a furniture store, Dupree stopped and sat on a wooden bench. The sun felt good on his legs and he got a whole new perspective as he looked above the awnings and signs at the upper floors of the buildings along Inspiration Street. Real estate, bookkeeping, and notary offices with small signs in the windows filled three of the spots directly across the street. Further down, there was a seamstress and a chiropractor.

"Are you lost?" a heavy-set boy with thick glasses asked, plopping down next to Dupree.

"I don't think so," Dupree said.

"You look lost." The boy stared at him waiting for a response.

The boy exhibited the characteristics of possessing an extra chromosome. His slightly almond eyes and thick tongue made Dupree pretty sure he was displaying the signs of Down syndrome.

"My name is Toby." The boy nodded, assuring Dupree it was true.

"I'm Dupree. Nice to meet you."

"This is my bench you know."

"I didn't know that. It's really comfortable."

"My dad bought it and put it here so I would have somewhere to sit while he is at work."

"Where does he work?"

Toby whirled around on the bench and pointed. "Are you stupid? Everybody knows my dad owns the furniture store!"

Dupree read the sign and said, "Oh, you're Toby Wharton!"

"Duh!" Toby replied loudly.

"Do you help your dad in the store?"

"No, he says I'm a screw-up and I break things. That's why he got me the bench. So I can stay outside and not break things."

"I see," Dupree said.

"Sometimes people sit with me on my bench, but most people don't."

"Is it okay if I sit here?" Dupree wasn't sure how to deal with Toby. He couldn't remember ever being close enough to a person with Down syndrome to talk to them. To be truthful, Dupree was surprised Toby could talk and make sense.

"Oh sure, you can sit here all you want."

"Thanks." The two sat side by side, not speaking for quite a while.

Dupree was a bit uncomfortable, but as the minutes passed he became more and more relaxed.

"I have to pee now, bye," Toby said, finally. He stood and Dupree watched him quickly go into the furniture store.

Dupree was about to leave too when a thin man with a thin mustache and narrow striped tie walked around the end of the bench.

"Are you Dupee?"

"Dupree? Yes, that's me.

"Jack Wharton, Wharton Furniture." The rather nervous man shot out his hand. "Was that kid of mine bugging you?"

"Not at all," Dupree said, shaking his hand.

"He thinks this bench is his. Sometimes he runs people off. Newcomers, you understand. Locals mostly won't sit here. Bad for business. These days you can't afford to lose sales. We're having a terrific sale on mattresses. All the big brands. If we don't have it we can order it. One year financing, no interest, same as cash, you see."

"Does Toby sit out here a lot?"

"Pretty much," Wharton said, nervously. "Not a lot for his kind to do around here, you understand. Small town people are funny. Lost a lot of friends when he was born, a lot of friends. People don't know what to do, you know. I get it, it's hard. You must be new in town, haven't seen you around."

"I just arrived today. Seems like a nice place."

"Just don't have a retarded kid. Might as well have leprosy. It's hard, you know, but I get it. People don't know what to say, how to act, I get it."

"Toby seems like a nice kid. How old is he?"

"Twenty-four. Yeah, he's getting' up there. Not a lot for him to do around here."

The man was so stressed and nervous Dupree couldn't imagine what a customer must think. How can he make a sale? he wondered.

"Been in the furniture business long?" Dupree asked, trying to get on a more comfortable subject.

"Third generation. My grandfather started the store in thirty-six. Good business. Love the furniture business. I do the books and ordering; my wife works the floor. She knows everybody, everybody loves my Karen. I kind of stay out of the way."

"Nice to have a legacy," Dupree offered, then instantly regretted it.

"Yeah, kinda, but Toby's an only child. My wife wanted to try again, but I said, 'Oh, hell no!' One's enough, you know what I mean. I mean, yeah, one is plenty. You got kids?"

"Two. I'll trade you straight across." Dupree didn't smile or look away from Jack Wharton.

"That's not funny," Wharton said.

"Not meant to be. I like Toby. Seems like a good kid."

"Well, the charm wears off, believe you me, the charm wears off."

Dupree stood and faced Wharton. "Sometimes people don't know how well off they are. When was the last time Toby hugged you?"

"Oh, sweet baby Jesus, he's always hugging on me or my wife. Sometimes, sometimes he even hugs the customers. We can't have that. Hugging customers." Wharton shook his head.

"Do they say anything? About the hugs, I mean."

"The locals don't say anything. New folks, sometimes they say something. They say it's sweet, but I think they're just saying it out of embarrassment."

"Does he ever tell you he loves you?"

"What are you, some kind of social worker or something? Why do you care? I don't abuse my kid!"

"I'm just asking. I got two kids that haven't told me they loved me or hugged me in years."

"He says it too much. I never told my dad I loved him ever, that I can remember. What kind of a boy says that all the time? Huh, I ask you. Not right. I don't think. Do you?"

"Why'd you come out here anyway, Mr. Wharton?"

"Just checkin', I can't have the boy running off customers."

"Well, I didn't run off." Dupree shrugged. "Tell Toby thanks for the use of his bench. I'll have to come back and chat with him again sometime. Nice boy."

Dupree walked straight across the street and didn't look back at the nervous little man. The idea of having a child who might have special needs never occurred to Dupree. He wished he had a child that would hug him. He couldn't remember when either of his kids hugged him. A few months ago he tried to put his arm around his daughter in the kitchen as he was leaving for work, just a normal sign of affection, just a simple side by side hug, just a quick father-daughter squeeze. She wriggled out of his embrace and squealed, "Oh, sick!"

Dupree scrambled from the house, feeling dirty and somehow at fault. He vowed he would never try to touch her again.

Chapter Three

"Martin Hutchinson, please." Diane hated going through a secretary. After all, her husband was a partner in the firm.

"Mr. Hutchinson's office. Katarina, how may I help?"

"Hi Katarina, is Marty in?"

"Who's calling?"

"You know damn good and well who's calling. Is he in?"

"One moment, please."

The music on hold seemed to be an additional insult to the humiliation of being asked who she was. Starting with Dupree's secretary, Diane seemed to have alienated all the clerical personnel she'd ever made contact with. She expected royal treatment.

There was a special relationship between the attorneys and their secretaries. They were the gatekeepers, the Rolodex, confidants, last-minute gift purchasers, and the ones who made the poor spelling and grammatical nightmares of their boss into briefs, reports, and petitions, and other documents into polished and orderly prose that otherwise would be a shambles.

Wives, on the other hand, were tolerated. Their petty jealousy, the condescending nature of their calls, and demanding interruptions to the flow of meetings and conferences with clients, and closed-door times of research and study must be handled with kid gloves. The wives of partners were even worse because of their belief that the position of their husbands gave them special significance. Of all the wives at Atherton, Miller, and Chase, Diane Dupree was the most hated.

"Good morning, Diane." Martin Hutchinson, by nature of his profession, was an Academy Award level actor, and as good a liar as any politician. Diane Dupree was his partner's wife, but he hated her as much as Dupree did, maybe more. The fact he himself could remain civil to her was a mystery to him, and an act that she was oblivious to.

"Where is he, Marty? He's called you, hasn't he? Did you hatch up some kind of scheme together?"

"I'm fine, thanks, Diane. How are you?" Hutchinson said in a mock sincerity that put a smile on his face.

"This is no time to be cute."

"Long past that, Diane. Here's what I know. He's not dead or kidnapped. Beyond that, I'm as in the dark as anyone else. Now is there something you need help with? Money, legal advice, do the kids need counseling?"

"I want a divorce," Diane barked.

"I'm not married to you. You'll have to take that up with your husband."

"Well. We don't know where he is, do we? Write it up, I'll sign it. I want half of everything!"

"In California that is your legal right."

"How much is his share of the firm?" Diane was firing the first shot in what could be a legal gang war.

"Atherton, Miller, and Chase is a California Legal Corporation. You know very well; Dupree is an employee of the corporation, as am I, thereby all assets of the firm are protected under State Corporate law."

"I didn't know that," Diane snapped.

"That's a shame," Hutchinson continued. "At the time of his disappearance, all current billing procedures and pending cases were divided among the other partners to be assigned to staff attorneys. Your real and personal properties are, as you are obviously aware, part of any divorce settlement."

"Are you saying that all his years at the firm are of no value?"

"Not in any legal proceedings. His shares are in a trust administered and controlled by an independent accounting firm for the protection of all partners against any kind of majority distribution, hostile or otherwise. So, until his death or hostile separation from this firm, all assets are in the control of Atherton, Miller, and Chase. It is basically our in-house retirement fund."

"Well, I want my share!"

"Frankly my dear, that is exactly why the fund was, and is, designed against such eventualities. You can try, but every law office I know of has something similar. The possibility of any attorney in this state fighting against their own self-interest and setting precedent against similar funds, it's just not in the cards."

"Auuuuuuugh!" Diane screamed into the phone. "Just write up the papers! I want shed of him now! Not Later!"

"I'm afraid I can't represent you. I can give you the names of some good divorce attorneys, but yours is a pretty cut and dry division of assets. Eric isn't a minor, so no support there. How old is Deanna now?"

"She's seventeen, eighteen in July," Diane snapped.

"That leaves a few months to go for her. If I were you, I would come to an amicable settlement, get child support for the months until July, and go your separate ways. It would save you a lot of time and money."

"Well, you can help me list the house without his signature at least?"

"As I said, I can't represent you. Dupree's my friend and partner. I can give you some sound advice and a couple of reminders. That is if you can calm down a bit." Hutchinson was tiring of the conversation and was just about to tell her where to go, but decided to twist the knife first.

"First of all, just maintain the status quo until you hear from Dupree. Don't do anything foolish you might regret later. Don't spend any money unnecessarily."

"I emptied all our accounts this morning and canceled the credit cards," she said defiantly.

"Diane, as a friend, I would advise against that, it is exactly what I am talking about. Fifty percent of all that means all assets will be divided equally. You do not want to find yourself in a position of paying back the money you have spent. Secondly, I must remind you, your house and cars are assets of the firm, and as such, are benefits of the employee. You cannot sell, transfer or in any way subject them to liens or encumbrances." Hutchinson sat rocking in his over-sized Moroccan leather office chair with a big smile on his face, waiting for his last salvo to sink in.

"Since when?" Diane sounded as if she took a punch to the gut.

"Since, well, the month before you moved in. You picked it, we paid for it, ergo, we own it. Aren't you aware of the nature of your personal finances at all?"

"I just sign when needed. What good is it to be married to a lawyer if you have to read everything?"

"Look." Hutchinson was ready for the knock-out punch. "If I were you I'd go down to the local Do it Yourself Legal Service office, spend $139, and get it all taken care of.

"Remember, any and all of your legal expenses come out of your half of the money. Speaking of that, I'd put all that money back. At least until you get papers drawn up, then just cut it in two." Hutchinson paused for effect, "If you need a reference for a new place let me know, I'll be happy to give you one."

"A new place? What do you mean?" Diane was now on the verge of tears. The reality of divorce from Dupree began to set in.

"If you're divorced, you can't stay in the house. Especially if he moves out. It will revert to the firm as a dispensable asset. Hey, I hate to cut this short, but I have a client waiting. We'll talk later." Hutchinson didn't wait for a good-bye, he just hung up.

Katarina looked up at the sound of her boss's laughter coming from behind the thick oak door. The door opened and Martin Hutchinson was wiping his eyes.

"My God that felt good," he chuckled with delight. "I don't care what; never put another call from that woman through again. You have my permission to make up the biggest whopper you can come up with about where I am or what I'm doing!"

"Yes, sir!" Katarina relished the thought of simply saying no to Diane Dupree.

A few miles away Diane threw the phone against the kitchen wall and burst into angry tears.

Dupree's second day in White Owl began with a hot shower. Instead of shaving, Dupree neatly trimmed his neck of five days' growth. He looked in the mirror at his salt and pepper beard. Still more pepper than salt, but he liked the look. His bruises were fading and the deep purple was now more of a gray. Instead of looking like he was beaten up, he looked more like he hadn't slept in a month. Without his normal regime of gels and conditioners, Dupree simply parted his hair on the side instead of the harsh, powerful, straight back style he normally wore.

He was on his way out when Grammy called from the kitchen. "Want a cup of coffee?"

"That would be nice." Dupree like her company and accepted happily.

"So where are you from, anyway?" she asked, as he seated himself at the kitchen table.

"Los Angeles. Costa Mesa, originally."

"I was born right here in this house. I went to Seattle on my honeymoon, and Tacoma for surgery on my gall bladder, but other than that I never been out of White Owl," Grammy said proudly. "So what made you ramble?"

"Thought it was time for a new start."

"I started over twice in my life. Once when I got married and once when my Russell died. Funny, both had to do with him. I sure miss that old rascal."

"How long has he been gone?" Dupree asked.

"Almost twenty years. Doesn't seem that long. The days go by and you look up and there's a new president, look up again they're gone. Time truly does fly. Just the same, it would have flown better with Russell."

"Do you have children?"

"No, the Lord never saw fit to bless us with any. Tried, Lord knows, we tried. Sure was fun tryin', but nothin' ever came of it. You?"

"Two, a boy and a girl. They are the product of their mother's hovering and smothering. They haven't got much use for me."

"That's too bad."

"It is what it is," Dupree replied. He paused for a moment, realizing that he actually felt sorry for them. "You know, I built a life based on a false narrative. I believed that the life I dreamed up could actually exist. Mine ended up like one of those old science fiction movies where the scientist creates the perfect robots. Then when they learn to think for themselves, they're evil and want the scientist dead.

"I picked the wife that looked the part, had the perfect job, had a boy and a girl, and a house in the suburb. All according to plan. I woke up a week ago and decided to kill myself. Then I thought, why give them the satisfaction, and like you said, I decided to ramble."

"You seem to me to be a pretty easy goin' fella."

"Amazing what a few hundred miles can do." Dupree took his last sip of coffee. "I think I'll try the café this morning and see if I can get acquainted with a few people, see if I can start networking, and find a job."

"Networking? Is that L.A. for something?"

"I guess it is. I'll just see who knows who, and see if the dots connect to something."

"Getting closer, but I guess it is a new kind of Tella system."

"You got it! Thank you for the coffee," Dupree said, standing.

"This is a nice simple town. What you see is what you get. You could start over a lot of worse places."

"I think 'simple' might just be the thing."

The eight o'clock breakfast crowd packed The Quarter Moon. Dupree stood at the counter looking around the room trying to find a seat or even a stool.

"Last seat left." A bald man in a booth called out. "If you ain't picky you can join us."

"Thanks." Dupree joined the three men in the booth. "I'm Dupree."

"Terry," the bald man said.

"Cal, and this is my brother Kenny." Both men nodded at once.

"Yeah, we're the Perry twins," Ken said shyly.

"So, what brings you to our fair city?"

"Looking for a nice place to live." Dupree smiled.

"That it is," Terry said. "Lookin' for work?"

"Yes, I am."

"What do you do?" Cal asked.

"Well, I've only done a couple different things. Fast food, working in a shoe store and..."

"You want fries with that?" Kenny teased.

"That was me," Dupree agreed.

Cal nodded his head encouraging Dupree to continue. "Then what?"

"I worked mostly." Dupree took a deep breath and decided to tell the whole truth. "I was a lawyer."

"No shit?" Terry exclaimed.

"Twenty-five years, more or less." Dupree looked around the table, "Nobody getting up?"

"I never met a lawyer before. I seen them on TV of course, but never like, I mean, like sittin' at the same table." Terry acted as if the Pope was sitting next to him.

"Then you, Terry my friend, are among the fortunate."

The four men laughed good-heartedly.

"You're what they call over-qualified for me," Kenny said, frowning.

"What do you do, Kenny?"

"Septic tanks, installed, pumped and dumped." The pride in his business was mixed with strong signals of inferiority.

"I think you might starve in White Owl being a lawyer."

"Yeah, we haven't had one since, Mr., oh, what was his name?"

"Mitchell."

"Yeah, since Mr. Mitchell died, and that's been several years ago now. His name is still up on a window above Olson's on Main Street."

"Good Morning. Back for more?" TJ approached the table.

"Yeah, I'd like a couple slices of that chocolate zucchini bread." Dupree grinned.

"That trick only works once."

"No, I will pay for it. I really liked it. And, uh, can I get a glass of milk, too?"

"Sure can, comin' right up." TJ spun around and was gone.

"Moves quick for such a big girl, don't she?" The twins laughed. Dupree wasn't sure which spoke. He let the remark go.

"So you got Dara's special yesterday, huh?"

"I guess so. Interesting tradition."

"Interesting woman. You see her yet?"

"No." Dupree wasn't sure where the conversation was going.

"Lovely," Kenny gushed.

"Lovely? What are you queer? Lovely? Oh, sorry I didn't mean anything if you were, you know." Terry grimaced and waited for a response from Dupree.

"No, I am not gay. If that's what you mean." Dupree looked at Kenny. "I think lovely is a good descriptive term. I've used it and I think it often is the best word possible."

"Well, he talks like a lawyer."

"Whatever word you use, she is one fine looking lady." Kenny tried to regain some of his lost dignity.

"I have never understood why she hasn't remarried. Sad deal all 'round," Cal said.

"Her mother-in-law tried to introduce me yesterday."

"Cathy? Oh, yeah, anything in pants over thirty and under sixty she tries to get Dara interested in. So far no dice."

"Well, I am ineligible anyway, married." Dupree held up his left hand.

"Oh, too bad. Being a lawyer could have given you a real leg up around here," Kenny said enthusiastically.

TJ set a plate with two slices of zucchini bread with a scoop of cream cheese and a tall glass of milk in front of Dupree.

"Now, Tammy Jo here, she don't care if you're married or not. That right, TJ?"

"Shut up Terry, your wife is on speed dial. Let's see what she thinks."

Cal and Kenny laughed and razzed Terry for a couple of minutes. Dupree worked on the cream cheese and bread.

The twins went silent and both looked at Dupree.

"There she is," Cal whispered.

Dupree turned and looked toward the counter. He didn't mean to, he knew it was rude, but he just stared. Behind the counter stood a tall, beautiful woman with black hair and a white forelock on the right side of her part.

"That's Dara, the owner of this place?" Dupree asked after a moment.

"The one and only."

His question was intentional. He needed to look away, but he turned back to see if she was still there. She was wearing a heavily starched, crisp, white, tuxedo shirt. It was tucked into a colorful print skirt with a wide silver and turquoise Navajo belt. She was olive-skinned which, by contrast with the pale citizens of White Owl, appeared darker than it really was. It was her smile that wouldn't let Dupree look away.

Dupree was from the land of the movie stars and a million wannabes. In L.A. beautiful women were everywhere, serving coffee at Starbucks, taking tickets at the movies, and serving you Caesar salad at a hundred and one restaurants. This woman was different.

As Dara chatted and joked with the men at the counter she would smile, letting her dazzling white teeth and deep dimples light up her face like a Madonna in a renaissance painting. The effect was mesmerizing, Dupree realized he was just staring, waiting for her to smile again, and turned back to the group.

"Lovely. It is absolutely the only word for her. You hit it dead on, Kenny, she is truly lovely." Dupree felt he said too much. "So, about work. Any thoughts?"

"Not with me. Sorry."

"Me either."

"I'm a one-truck pooper scooper trooper," Kenny said.

"I'll ask around." Terry offered.

"The festival is coming up in a couple months," Cal offered.

"That's just temporary. You want real work, right?" Terry asked.

"Yeah, if I'm going to stay, I need regular employment. If not, I'll need to find someplace else I can earn a living. But I really think I'd like to stay here for a while."

"Now that you've seen Dara," Terry added, raising his eyebrows up and down in a lecherous Groucho Marx impersonation.

"Funny," Dupree said without expression. He picked up the glass of milk and finished it off. "I'll see you guys later. He reached in his pocket and tossed a dollar bill on the table."

"Heavy tipper. TJ's gonna love you," Cal remarked.

Dupree walked to the counter. He was praying that Dara would take his money. It was foolish, and he was embarrassed to admit to himself that he wanted a closer look. He wanted to hear her voice. Suddenly he wanted nothing more in the world.

He nervously touched both the mints and toothpicks sitting next to the register.

"Three fifty," TJ said, coming around the counter.

Dupree handed her five dollars, sneaking another glance at Dara.

"So, how'd you get on with the twins and Terry?"

"Great, nice guys."

"They tease hard but they'd give you the shirt off their backs."

"But not a job."

"A job? The only one who's worked in months is Kenny. Septic tanks are always fillin' up." TJ laughed. "The other two are just like most of the fellas around here. Nothin' to do but hang out in here until lunchtime. Then they go home. Kind of sad."

"Yeah, sure is." Dupree agreed. "Thanks, TJ, I'll see you tomorrow."

"I'll be here."

Dara was moving toward the register, but Dupree already said good-bye and couldn't think of a reason to stay. He turned toward the door.

"He's new," Dara said.

"Yeah, second day. Kind of handsome. If you can get past the black eyes."

"I didn't get a good look," Dara said, watching Dupree walk across the street.

"He sure likes your chocolate zucchini bread. Ordered it again today."

"Huh."

Inspiration Street's not awake yet, Dupree thought, as he tried to locate Olson's Stationery. He knew it was across the street from the furniture store but wasn't sure how far. Toby waved and yelled hello from the bench as Dupree walked by. Dupree looked at his watch. Eight-thirty. How many hours a day does that poor kid sit there? he thought as he spotted Olson's sign hanging under the eaves.

Dupree cupped his hands and tried to spot some form of life inside the darkened store.

"We don't open 'til ten." Dupree turned to see a man in a beige apron standing by a car at the curb.

"Wow, I didn't hear you pull up," Dupree said in surprise.

"Prius, it's in stealth mode. What can I help you with?"

"You must be Mr. Olson." Dupree waited for a response. There was none. "I was wondering what you could tell me about the old law office above your store."

"What do you want to know?" Olson was not friendly like the guys at the café.

"Is it rented? If not, how much? Stuff like that."

"Hell, I'd pay somebody to sit in there and chase kids out of the building. They run up and down the hall stomping as hard as they can. I can never get up there quick enough to catch them. I lock the fire exit but they're always cutting off the lock."

"Huh."

"What do you want it for?" Olson asked.

"I might open a law office."

"It's two rooms, reception, and office. The bathroom's down the hall. What's it worth to you?"

"I have no idea. No clients, yet. What does office space go for around here?"

"No tellin', most offices are owner-occupied, they rent out the storefronts below. How about a hundred bucks a month? With the agreement, you kill any kids you see up there."

"How about I just maim them?"

"Works for me." Olson finally smiled, then extended his hand. "Peter Olson."

"Dupree."

"Nice to meet you. The place is full of law books and stuff. Lot of files. You throw out what you can't use and I'll knock off a month's rent. Deal?"

"I'll be back at ten. If it looks good, you got a deal."

"Then I better dig out the key."

Ten minutes later, Dupree returned with a hundred dollars and a smile. Olson sent him upstairs alone with the keys. The door was framed in oak. The center of the door was pebbled glass. It looked more like Sam Spade should reside there, not an attorney.

The deadbolt gave a heavy metallic click as Dupree opened the door. Inside, the office was like a throwback to the seventies. The furniture was vintage chrome and Naugahyde. There were two chairs, a small table stacked with magazines, and a receptionist's desk that was void of anything that would indicate it was ever used. The desk didn't even have a chair behind it.

Mr. Mitchell's taste, if he indeed decorated the place, ran to cheap wood paneling, taxidermy ducks, and airline travel posters, giving the place a subliminal undertone suggesting if you fly United, you're a dead duck.

The door into the main office was standing slightly ajar. Knowing the previous occupant died while still in practice gave Dupree an uneasy voyeuristic kind of guilt entering a brother attorney's office. The scene was so perfect that it was like Mr. Mitchell stepped down the hall to use the restroom.

His coffee mug was sitting on the file folder on the corner of the desk. A law book and a yellow pad lay in the center of the desk, undisturbed. Dupree walked around the desk and ran his hand over the seat of the chair in an attempt to dust it off a little before he sat down.

As he pulled the chair up to the desk, Dupree spotted the desk calendar. Thursday, October 15, 2008, was the date of the exposed page. In pencil, Mitchell wrote, Call Judge Caldwell, Lunch 12:30 Fred, and call Lucy tonight. Dupree flipped though the yellow pad. The notes were neat, well organized, and the penmanship was tight, crisp, and clear. I could have learned a thing or two from this guy, he thought, as he put down the pad.

The walls were decorated with a variety of pictures and professional and community service awards. As he spun around in the chair, Dupree spotted a row of diplomas on the wall. Anthony John Mitchell, Bachelor of Arts History, Iowa State University, a law degree from the University of Chicago, and a Master's

Degree in Economics from Iowa State. What was he doing in this tiny town? Dupree thought.

"What are you doing here, is a better question," Dupree said aloud.

Across the room were five file cabinets. Three made of wood on the left of the door and two metal cabinets to the right. All five were covered with stacks of files. A leather couch covered the length of the far wall. It was sagging and the leather was cracked. It showed evidence of being slept on more than once.

The desk drawer on the top right was stuck, so Dupree jerked it back and forth before it let loose and opened. Just desk junk, he thought. The bottom drawer contained two dress shirts, freshly laundered, folded, and in clear plastic bags. Dupree picked them up and found a partial bottle of Wild Turkey and a Penthouse magazine.

The drawers on the opposite side were packed with file folders in hanging frames. He pulled a file at random, 1996. He pulled another, 1993. Reaching deep in the drawer he scooped out a large stack of the folders and plopped them down on the desk. All the folders were dated twenty years or older. The cabinets across the room contained the same vintage files.

Dupree took an armload of the folders and went to find the back door. Down an outside flight of stairs sat a big green dumpster. He threw the first armload in. For the next hour or so, Dupree would grab as many old files as he could manage and take them down to the dumpster. About a half-hour in, Peter Olson came up to check what was going on.

"You really want the free month!" Olson said, following Dupree to the Dumpster with an armload of his own. "How many trips have you made?"

"Lost track," Dupree said breathlessly, throwing a load into the dumpster.

"You are welcome to it!" Olson said, adding his stack to the pile. "I'm going back where I belong. Have fun."

The multiple trips to the dumpster, the countless steps that accompanied them, and being in less than peak physical shape were taking their toll on Dupree. At the one hour mark, he gave up and went in and dropped on the couch in the office. He didn't dare close his eyes or he would surely go to sleep, so he stared up at the ceiling, trying to formulate his plans for the new office.

After about five minutes he thought he heard a noise in the hall. He dismissed the sound to the creaky couch. Moments later he heard another sound. As quietly as the couch would allow, he stood and walked to the front office. The door was open to make going in and out easier. He heard something in the hall. This time he was sure. He moved to the door and, through the crack just above the center hinge, he saw a head of sandy blond hair scurry pass.

Dupree shot around the door and yelled, "Hey, hold on!"

A boy of about twelve was running up the hall.

"Hey wait a minute! You want to earn some money?" Dupree yelled again.

The body froze in his tracks. He slowly turned around and said, "Serious?"

"Yeah, I need some help. You got any friends outside?"

"Yeah," the boy replied.

"Go get them and come to my office."

Dupree went back into the inner office, sat down, and put his feet up on the desk. It wasn't long before the boy and two friends came through the door.

"I'm Dupree. What are your names?"

"I'm Heath." The boy in the hall spoke first.

"I'm Zack."

"I'm not sure we should be in here," the third boy said, looking Dupree directly in the eyes.

"That's a long name, what can I call you for short?" Dupree asked.

"His name is Steven," Zack said.

"Well, Steven, here is the deal. All these cabinets are full of paper. All that paper needs to go to the dumpster. I'll give you guys twenty bucks apiece when the job's done."

"Let's see the money," Steven said.

"Look, I'm the lawyer around here. You really think I'm going to stiff you for a lousy sixty bucks?"

"I'll do it!" Zack said.

"Me too. If Steven doesn't work can we split his twenty?" Heath asked.

"Who said I'm not workin', I'm just making sure we don't get gypped out of the money."

"Soon as you get started, the sooner you get paid. Now listen," Dupree stood. "You can't leave a mess. Anything you drop, you pick up. Empty the cabinets, all the drawers. No mess, got it? When you're done, there won't be a scrap of paper anywhere. Agreed? Outside too! In the dumpster!"

"Yes, sir!" Zack gave a mock salute.

"No mess, got it!" Heath agreed.

"What if it blows away?"

"Shut up, Steven! Then you go pick it up."

"Okay, get to work," Dupree commanded.

Each boy went to a cabinet, pulled out a drawer, scooped up a handful of folders, and ran for the dumpster. This process continued for three rounds. Then Zack walked his load out. Heath ran partway but took longer getting back. Steven's ego would not let him stop running with the other boys, but by the fifth load, he was walking too.

The boys tried a variety of processes for taking out the files. For a while they split the distance to the dumpster into thirds and, like loading watermelons, Heath took files from the drawer to Steven who ran them to Zack. This worked pretty well until Zack realized he was doing all the running up and down the stairs, and they went back to individual work. At one thirty-three the boys walked up to Dupree's desk and said they completed the task.

"Ready for inspection?"

"What do you mean?" Heath asked.

"I'm going to check for any mess or loose sheets of paper."

Steven turned and ran from the room. The other two just looked at each other.

In a couple of minutes, Steven returned. "Ready for inspection!"

Dupree smiled and went to the cabinet, pulling them open one by one. He walked down the hall and out the door.

"Nice job, guys!" Dupree proclaimed. "Now for the fun part! Is there a market nearby?"

"Big D around the corner," Zack said.

"Okay, here." Dupree handed each boy a five-dollar bill.

"Hey, you said twenty!" Steven squealed.

"It isn't your pay. I want you to go to the store and find the biggest container, jug, bottle, whatever, full of sticky, icky, staining, gross, greasy stuff you can find and bring it back. The one who spends the closest to the five bucks will get an extra surprise. Off you go. And hurry back, I'm hungry and want to go to lunch."

The boys ran down the alley with renewed strength. Steven was the first to return. He was struggling with a five-gallon container with a lid on it. It was way too heavy for a boy his size, but he would not be beaten.

"I think I win," he said proudly.

"What have you got there?" Dupree asked from where he sat on the stairs.

"I went to the Frosty Drive-in. I got a whole bucket of dirty oil from the deep fryer. It is greasy and stinky."

"What'd you spend?"

"That's the best part! Nothing! My sister works there and she gave it to me. Here is your money back!" Steven announced proudly.

"Brilliant!" Dupree laughed. "You can keep it!"

"Awesome!"

A moment later, Heath arrived pushing a shopping cart, with five-gallon jugs of fruit punch in it.

"I spent all but a nickel!" Heath declared. "Do I win?"

"We'll see. Where's Zack?"

"I don't know, he ran off when we got to the street."

Dupree and the boys sat for almost ten minutes before a pickup truck pulled up to the dumpster.

"There he is!"

Zack hopped out of the passenger side of the truck all smiles. A tall man with a huge beard and a shaved head came around from the driver's side.

"Hi, Zack! Who's this?" Dupree called out, standing up.

"My dad. He kind of is helping me."

"Hi, I'm Tyler," the man said. "Zack said you needed something that was sticky and would stain?"

"That's right. What have you guys got?"

"About a hundred pounds of old wine barrel sludge. You want it?"

"Wonderful! What did you spend, Zack?"

"He offered me five bucks for as much sludge as I would give him. I figured this was a fair amount!" Tyler said.

"Do I win?"

"You know, I think it is a three-way tie. You guys are amazing!"

"Here is what we are going to do. All those papers you hauled out here are people's private business. They may be real old but they still might have stuff in them that people don't want known. So, we are going to pour all of your contributions all over them!"

The boys began shouting and pumping their fists in the air.

"What a mess!"

"Greasy! Greasy! Greasy!"

"Now listen up. I don't want your moms coming down here yelling at me about you ruining your clothes, so what if I do the pouring?"

"Cool," Steven said. "My mom would kill me if I ruined my shirt."

"I'll take care of Zack's portion," Tyler offered, walking to the back of the truck.

A few minutes later, Tyler and Dupree had poured and dumped all the oil, sludge, and fruit punch over the small mountain of folders. Tyler got a shovel out of his truck and stirred up the dumpster.

"Yuck!" one of the boys shouted.

"I think that will discourage anybody from digging in those papers, what do you think guys?"

"I'm not getting' in there!" Heath grimaced.

"OK. Time to pay up." Dupree reached in his pocket and pulled out three twenty-dollar bills.

"Oh, before I give you your very hard-earned money, I have a favor to ask of all of you."

"What?" Steven asked first.

"It seems some kids have been cutting the lock off the back door up there and running up and down the hall, making all kinds of racket. Can you guys keep a lookout and make sure they don't do it anymore? If they turn out to be bigger than you, you let me know and I'll take care of it, deal?"

The three boys looked at each other without saying a word. Dupree looked at Tyler and he gave a wink.

"It's a deal. We'll be like private security from now on. No need to worry," Steven volunteered.

Dupree passed out the twenty's and shook hands with each of the boys.

"I think I'm going to like this town. You got some pretty cool people around here," Dupree said with a big smile. "Now, I have got to get something to eat!"

"Come on guys, I'll give you all a ride home," Tyler said, more of an order than an offer.

"Come visit the brewery sometime. I'd love to give you a tour. First bottle's always free," Tyler said, shaking Dupree's hand.

"I must do that. If you ever need any legal work, you know where I am. At least Zack does."

"Nice to meet you. Welcome to White Owl. I think you're gonna fit right in."

The boys jumped in the cab talking a hundred miles an hour about what they were going to do with their newfound wealth.

"Thanks, Dupree!" Steven yelled from the window of the truck as it pulled away.

"That kid would make a great lawyer," Dupree said, watching the truck go down the alley.

"What the hell is all that mess!"

Dupree looked up to see Peter Olson at the top of the stairs.

"Hi Pete, somebody poured a bunch of nasty stuff all over the files!"

"Good thing they pick up Monday! What a stench!"

"We'll have to keep the door closed."

"And locked! Here's a new padlock. Next one, you buy."

"Sounds fair to me." Dupree smiled, reaching the top of the stairs. "I don't think I'm going to ever need to buy another."

"That so?"

"That's so," Dupree agreed.

Chapter Four

The Quarter Moon Café seemed peaceful as Dupree approached. There were only three cars now parked in front instead of the eight work trucks at the breakfast hour. In the corner of the front window was a help wanted sign. Dupree couldn't remember it being there earlier. He opened the door to the airy tinkle of a bell's welcome, again something that he didn't hear earlier. It was a completely different atmosphere than breakfast. The Quarter Moon was at peace, no rowdy breakfast chatter. Inside he found peace and quiet instead of the working man's diner. Several couples were having a quiet lunch. What a difference a few hours make, he thought.

Dupree approached the sign in the window and looked around. TJ was busy filling salt and pepper shakers at the counter. The people eating lunch didn't even notice that he arrived. He picked up the sign and walked to the counter. Behind him, he heard the bell above the door. He turned and saw Dara coming in with a grocery bag.

Panic suddenly hit Dupree. Silly as it seemed, he was terrified to speak to the café owner. She put the bag on the corner of the counter and shot TJ an angry look.

"Are you being helped?" There was that incredible smile.

Dupree felt like a speechless love-struck sixteen-year-old as he held up the Help Wanted sign and returned her smiled with a goofy grin.

"Seriously?"

"Is the position still open?"

"Well, yes but…"

"Then I would like to be interviewed. Apply, at the very least." Dupree spoke with the confidence of a battle-tested attorney.

"Who put you up to this?" Dara was no longer smiling.

"No one. I need part-time work. It is part-time, isn't it?"

"If you're serious, which I'm still doubtful of, what is it you think I need somebody for?"

"Anything but cook, and I feel I am fully capable of managing."

"Alright, well I don't need a cook. I need a busboy. Ours ran off with Chloe Parker last night. Do you know the Parkers?"

"No, I'm new in town. I really didn't know anyone yet. I've met Cathy and Carl and they are very nice. I'm staying with Grammy Morrow until I get settled. Oh, and Peter rented me office space above his store. I met Tyler, the brewery owner, and his boy Zack and his friends Heath and Steven. I met a pair of twins this morning at breakfast." Dupree paused.

"Anybody else?"

"Oh, yeah, the guy that owns the furniture store and his son, Toby."

"But other than that, you don't know anybody, huh? That's like a fourth of the town!" Dara laughed. "I'm Dara, I own this place."

"I'm Dupree."

"Okay Dupree, so you need part-time work and you rented office space."

"Right."

"What do you need office space for?"

"I intend to practice law here."

"You're a lawyer, and you want to be my busboy?"

"Not for life, just till I start getting a few clients."

"And use the café to meet everybody in town sooner or later."

"That wouldn't hurt either."

"What happened to your nose, and no B.S."

"I got mugged."

"Where are you from?"

"L.A. area."

"Why White Owl?"

"I met a kid on a bus bench in California who said the people here were cool and the Summer Music Festival was worth taking in. I don't know, I needed a destination, and it sounded as good as anywhere. Now that I've been here a couple of days I kind of like it."

"And you would seriously work here as a busboy?"

"Why not?"

"First off, it is called a busboy. You are far from that. Second, it is hard work, you do the whole café by yourself, and load and empty the dishwasher.

Third, and the one I am stuck on is, it isn't very dignified. And frankly, you don't strike me as the invisible, compliant, plate scraping type."

"You've got me there. This would certainly be a departure from my usual activities."

"Look, Mr. Dupree, you seem to be a nice guy. But I can't see this working. So, I'm going to have to say no. I hope there are no hard feelings."

"How could I possibly jeopardize my standing with the woman who makes the most incredible chocolate zucchini bread I ever tasted?" Dupree smiled, almost relieved at her declining his application.

"Charmer," Dara said coyly.

"I have another idea," Dupree began.

"No, I won't go out with you."

"I'm flattered, but that's not what I was going to say." Dupree could have sworn Dara's cheeks reddened. "Do you know Toby Wharton?"

"I know the poor kid sits on that bench in front of his folk's furniture store all day and half the night."

"Why not hire him?"

"Right, a poor mental, whatever the proper name for it is kid that just sits on a bench. That is an even worse idea than hiring you." Dara smiled and shook her head. "You really are a lawyer."

"What if you didn't have to pay him?" Dupree offered.

"That wouldn't be fair, to take advantage," Dara said indignantly.

"Absolutely. No argument there. What I said was, what if you didn't have to pay him. There are all kinds of state and federal programs that pay for the training of the handicapped."

"Everybody in town hates Wharton. You'd never get him to agree to 'exposing' his son to the stares of the town's people. Have you met him?"

"He's pretty unpleasant, and his attitude about his son's condition is from the dark ages. Let me handle him." Dupree took a deep breath. "If I make the calls, line up a training program that will pay all or half of Toby's wages, and he is willing and able to carry out his duties to your satisfaction, would you consider hiring him?"

"Have you ever lost a case?" Dara asked, grinning at Dupree.

"Once or twice."

"If you can line it up, and get past Wharton, I would be willing to talk to him. No promises."

"None expected."

"You really never intended to work here, did you?"

"Not really. I would have if you said yes, but I was really thinking of Toby."

"So, why the charade?"

"Ah, you always have to build your case by gently tearing down any possible objection to your real purpose by the deflection and misdirection of the opposition."

"Welcome to White Owl, Mr. Dupree. We must have a cup of coffee sometime. I think the rest of your story may be worth hearing."

"Just Dupree, and thank you. I'll take you up on the coffee if it comes with zucchini bread." Dupree was completely at ease with Dara. The look in her eyes was something he was not used to seeing. Truth. Her smile came from a place of sincerity; it was as real as her home-baked goods from the kitchen.

"Deal."

"I guess I better go arrange for a phone. Thanks for having an open mind."

"Thank you for having a big heart."

"That, my dear, I have never been accused of before." Dupree stood and gave her a melancholy smile.

"Things change. I know." Dara didn't smile. She picked up her shopping bag and said, "Have a nice day."

"You too," and Dupree meant it.

The next three days Dupree busied himself, setting up his office, buying a few things he needed that Mitchell didn't leave in the office. He arranged to get a phone and Internet service, opened a bank account, and ordered business cards from Olson's.

On the third day, he contacted the Washington Bar Association and requested the paperwork to transfer his law license. There were a few hurdles to get over, but he was express-mailed a temporary permit to practice law in Washington and assured it was just a matter of filing the right documents, all of which could be done on the Internet.

The missing ingredient was a computer. Dupree looked at Olson's meager offerings and decided there must be another way. On his way to lunch on the third day, he spotted Toby sitting on his bench with a laptop computer. He hadn't seen him in a couple of days and was concerned that he may have gotten the boy in some kind of trouble.

"Hi Toby, I missed seeing you."

"I went to grandma's house."

"Nice. Where does she live?" Dupree asked.

"Kirkland. It is far away. I threw up in the car. I get car sick easy."

"What have you got here?"

"My grandma gave me it. It is a computer. I am having a hard time with it."

"Can I see?"

"Sure. You know what to do? Play some games. No guns though. I like nice games." Toby handed Dupree the computer.

"Let's take a look. Wow, it's a nice one, Toby."

Dupree quickly searched for any games that might be installed. The only thing he could find was solitaire and a slot machine game. Not exactly the kind of thing Toby wanted. To Dupree's surprise, he saw the Wi-Fi logo blinking. He clicked it on and found Olson's Internet connection was unsecured, and providing a strong signal. With a double click, Dupree was on the net.

"Do you know any games you like?"

"Funny Farm, it has animals. Oh, and Mario, I like Mario, can you get Mario?" Toby was growing excited and animated with the prospect of having games to play.

Dupree logged onto his Amazon account and searched for video games. Within minutes he downloaded six games to Toby's laptop, all of which doubled as learning programs.

"There you go, buddy. I got you six games. Now, can I get something for me?"

"Sure you are my best friend, you can get whatever you want! Do you like games too?"

"Actually," Dupree said, typing in a search for computers, "I need a laptop too."

It only took a moment or two to find the same make and model as he left in L.A. He changed the delivery address and hit continue to purchase. His credit card information was declined.

"Great."

"You find a good one?" Toby asked, leaning over to watch Dupree work on the order.

"I thought I did. Let's see here." Dupree stood and took his wallet out of his pocket. "Time for my James Bond never be taken alive credit card lifeline!"

"Is that your favorite game?" Toby asked excitedly.

"I think it might be," Dupree answered with a smile.

He punched in the numbers of the card from his wallet. It was a debit card from his secret account. He entered the PIN and the transaction was complete. Arrival date, twenty-four hours.

"Do you need some help getting your games started?" Dupree asked.

"You better help."

Dupree double-clicked the icon of a smiling cow, and Funny Farm exploded onto the screen.

"Funny Farm! Funny Farm!" Toby clapped his hands. "I can do this one! I know how."

"Toby?" A woman's voice called.

"Hi, mom! Look what Dupee did. He got me games! Look!"

"That's nice, honey." A well-dressed woman of around fifty stepped around the bench. Her expression was one of polite concern. "And you are?"

"Hi, I'm Dupree," he said, standing. "Toby and I have been getting acquainted. I'm new in town and just rented the office above Olson's Stationery. I met your husband a few days ago. Nice to finally meet you."

"What's this about games?" Her tone was full of accusations.

"I downloaded some educational games for Toby from Amazon. The only thing we could find on his laptop was Solitaire and that didn't seem appropriate. He was nice enough to let me order something from Amazon, so I returned the favor by getting him some games. I hope you don't mind."

"No, I suppose not." She still seemed cautious. "I'm Karen Wharton, I'm sorry."

"I've been wanting to talk to you about something. Have you got a minute?" Dupree smiled.

"As long as no one goes in the store."

"Great. Toby, are you okay with that game?"

"Yes, yes, I know this one."

Dupree moved away from the bench and closer to the front doors of the store. "I hope you don't mind, but I spoke with Dara at The Quarter Moon Café last week about the possibility of Toby working there as a busboy."

"Why would you do that?" Karen asked harshly.

"Well, frankly, because I like the kid, and he seems bored to death sitting on that bench all day."

"I can't see that is any of your concern."

"It really isn't. I saw their help wanted sign and immediately thought of Toby. I made a deal with Dara, that with your permission, I would arrange with the State of Washington to get Toby into a training program that would pay his wages and enroll him in the job training and counseling program. It teaches life skills and self-sufficiency. It is truly a great program."

"Why are you asking me and not his father?" Karen Wharton was as stoic as stone.

"Frankly, I didn't think he would see the merits. I think he has some feelings that are hard for him to deal with concerning Toby. I was hoping that you might understand the importance of Toby getting out and being able to adjust to the world around him."

Karen Wharton whirled around and threw her hands up to her face. Her slender shoulders shook. It was clear to Dupree she was crying. He went and sat back down next to Toby. The young man was so engaged in the game he didn't even notice Dupree returning.

As he watched Toby play Funny Farm, he began to wonder if perhaps he was expecting too much. The game was about kindergarten, maybe the first-grade level. Could Toby do the busboy job? He's a friendly, seemingly happy guy sitting on his bench, but what would the pressure of working in the café do to him? How would he deal with people? How would the people of White Owl deal with him?

"Mr. Dupree," Karen softly called.

He went to where she stood.

"I'm sorry for my reaction. We, that is Toby and me, are isolated from people because of my husband's attitude and behavior sometimes. He can be so harsh. He doesn't think before he speaks. He blames me, he blames God, he is just so hurt and disappointed that Toby is, well you know. He wasn't always like that. Since Toby was born he's changed, turned inward. Sometimes he is so angry. I have left him twice." Karen sniffed and wiped her eyes. "My greatest fear is what will happen to Toby when I die. My husband will put Toby in a home of some kind if I go first, and not look back. I can't stand the thought of that happening. Can you really help him?"

"I think so. He will need to go and talk to Dara, kind of interview. The teachers from the State will help him with the job. They will actually shadow him, come alongside him and work with him, until is he confident to do things on his own. Then they will monitor his progress. Their goal is independent living for people with special needs."

"Why are you doing this?" Karen Wharton's chin was quivering and her eyes were welling up with tears.

"If I had a son like Toby, I would want him to get everything the world has to offer, to make him happy, and have a sense of acceptance and self-worth. When I saw him on the bench the first time, he asked me if I was lost. Right then I knew there was something special about him. It probably sounds crazy, but I am trying to start fresh from a life that was completely self-centered. I was kind of like your husband.

I was full of anger and self-hate. Then I decided there must be a better way. Let's just say that Toby is my first step in coming back."

"I think God sent you to us. I am at the end of my rope. I don't know where to turn. I don't want pity or anything like that. I just want to talk to an adult who isn't full of rage, or that doesn't have the mental capacity of a ten-year-old. Is that selfish?"

"You just need space. A break. I get it. Let's get you some help, too."

"What if Jack won't go along?"

"That is a different problem. You will have some hard choices then."

"No, I don't think it will be that hard this time." Karen seemed to stand a little straighter. "So what do we do?"

"I think talking to Toby comes first. Without him, the whole thing kind of falls apart. Do you think he'll be interested?"

"Will you help me talk to him?"

"If you want." Dupree wasn't sure if it was the right thing or not, but he agreed. "How about we do it tomorrow about this time? He's having way too much fun, it would be difficult, I'm sure, for him to be torn away right now."

"You're probably right, tomorrow it is then."

"I'll see you tomorrow, Toby!" Dupree called out.

"Wait! Wait! Wait!" Toby set the laptop down on the bench, jumped up and ran to where Dupree stood. He threw his arms around Dupree's middle and locked him in a bear hug. "Thank you for the games, Dupee, you are my best friend!"

"Okay, you're welcome!" Dupree said breathlessly. "You're welcome, glad you like them."

"Okay Toby, that's enough," Karen said gently.

"He is my friend mom!"

"I know, sweetheart, he's my friend too."

Toby let go as quickly as he took hold and returned to his game.

"Stronger than he looks!" Dupree smiled.

The walk to The Quarter Moon felt good. Dupree felt good to help someone without the expectation of reward. To his delight, if nothing else happened, he got the reward of a bone-crushing hug. Dupree smiled at the thought of Toby's reaction to the games. The lot at the café was empty. As he approached the door, two women were leaving.

"Something needs to be done."

"But what?"

"I don't know, but that's just not right."

"You want to go back in, just in case?"

"No, let's just get back to work."

The tension inside the café was palpable. The silence was unnatural for the ordinarily, cheerful place. The bell didn't sound above his head. Dupree glanced up and the curved hook was gone, along with the bell, and there were raw open wounds in the wood where the screws were ripped out.

TJ was at the far end of the room standing perfectly still. Her eyes flashed towards Dara when she saw Dupree. Dara was standing behind the counter. In her left hand was a miniature baseball bat like they give out on fan appreciation day. Her knuckles were white from her grip on it.

Dara looked at Dupree. Her bright eyes normally so full of light and life were dark with fear. She turned and Dupree followed her gaze to a man sitting with his back against the wall. He leaned back in his chair and one large boot rested on the table.

Without hesitation, Dupree jovially walked to where Dara stood behind the counter, gave her a big kiss on the cheek and said, "How's it going, sweetie?"

"What's goin' on here?" the man growled.

"I was about to ask the same," Dupree said brightly.

Dupree slapped Dara on the bottom and said, "How about some banana nut bread, cutie. I'm starvin'."

"Who is this clown?" the man asked, slamming both feet to the floor. "What's all this sweetie cutie shit?"

"Hey, now." Dupree turned on the stool. "That is in violation of the language policy of this fine establishment. Didn't you see the sign on the door?"

The man stood. His posture was angry and threatening. "I asked who you were and I expect an answer."

"You first. After all, you were here first."

"Damn right, I was here first. First in town, first in this building, and first in line for her."

"Is that right?" Dupree turned back to Dara. "Is that right? That's a lot of firsts."

"He's got two out of three right." Dara's voice was missing her usual sparkle.

"Okay, so you seem to be a little grouchy. Did TJ get your order wrong?" Dupree's tone seemed to grate on the man. Flashes across his eyes made it very clear he was angry, and with the addition of Dupree in the mix, confused and frustrated. "Let's start over. I'm Dupree. Are you going to get my nut bread, angel?"

Dara laid the mini bat on the counter and said, "Oh, I forgot. You want milk or coffee?"

"You know I always have milk." Dupree smiled and gave her an almost imperceptible nod toward the kitchen. "I'm sorry, what did you say your name was?"

"Slader. Why have I never seen you around here?"

"I've been in L.A. I moved to be closer to Dara. Great little town here."

"I think you're full of shit. You're not funny, clever, or charming. I don't know what your game is, but Dara and I have an understanding. When the time comes for her to stop grieving and be with a man again, it will be me. So your playacting is thin as tissue. She doesn't want you, or anybody like you. I have been waiting for nearly fifteen years, since the first time I came in here. She knows my intent, and I will not take no for an answer. The problem is, I am growing tired of waiting."

"Why is it I get the impression she's tired of you?" Dupree was no longer smiling. His bluff was getting dangerously close to being called. He was not a fighter, the man facing him was.

The kitchen door swung open. Dara returned with a loaf of nut bread, a glass of milk, and a butcher's knife.

"Travis, it is time for you to go." Dara was emboldened and her voice showed anger and contempt.

"Not 'til you apologize for lettin' this guy paw on you."

"Maybe I like it. Maybe I like him. Maybe you and your unwanted attention has reached the point of being disgusting and embarrassing. I have tried to be nice, I've tried not to be mean. But I am sick of you coming in here frightening my customers and my staff and it is going to stop. I am not interested in you. I don't like you."

Dara rounded the counter. She pointed at the sign above the kitchen door with the butcher's knife. "In all the years I have run this place I have never had to use this, but I am using it now. I reserve the right to refuse service to anyone. That anyone is you. You are refused service starting here and now. If you ever darken that door again I will have you arrested for trespass. Am I clear?"

"What are you going to do, call the cops?" Slader laughed.

"I'll call the governor if I have to!"

"You pickin' him over me?" Travis growled.

"I would pick almost anybody I can think of over you. Now get out!" Dara's last words were an angry shout.

"This isn't over. You are mine. You get it? I will not let anybody have you."

"It is not your choice!" Dara screamed.

Dupree stood and picked up the mini bat. He was in way over his depth. He already knew what a broken nose felt like. He lived through it; he would do it again if it meant freeing Dara from this unwanted suitor. His mind raced with the legalities of clubbing someone with a miniature baseball bat. More likely was the proposition that Travis would be locked up for beating him to death. To his eternal gratefulness, Travis turned toward the door.

As he grasped the doorknob, Travis turned one last time, "You're a dead man." Travis's words spit out in rage. He turned and left The Quarter Moon Café.

"What were you thinking?" Dara yelled as the door slammed shut.

"I'm not quite sure. You were in some kind of trouble and I did the only thing that came to my mind." Dupree shrugged sheepishly.

"He could have killed you. He's crazy! For heaven's sake!" Dara turned and put her hands on her hips. Her head was down as she stared at the floor. After a long moment she turned back around, her composure somewhat intact. "I'm sorry. Thank you."

"You're welcome."

"I think you're as crazy as he is! But in a good way."

Dara and Dupree burst into relieved laughter.

"But, I swear to God, if you ever slap my butt again I'll cut your hand off!" She picked up the butcher's knife and dramatically chopped the loaf of banana nut bread in two.

"I will remember that." Dupree smiled nervously, and they both laughed again.

"I don't see what's so funny," TJ said, approaching the laughing pair.

"Me either!" Dara said, going into fits of laughter again.

A short while later, Dupree left the café for his office without eating anything. He saw Toby on the other side of the street, but he was glued to his laptop and didn't pay any attention. There was a notice on the door when he got to the office. The phone company tried to install the phone but no one was there. They would return tomorrow.

Dupree went in and sat at his desk. He replayed the scene in the café several times. Each time he became more heroic. Each time the kiss was more passionate and on Dara's wine red lips. Each time the slap on the bottom became more of a daring embrace.

"What are you doing?" Dupree asked himself, spinning around in his chair. "You're married. She's, she's, she's whatever she is, and it doesn't include you." He glared at his reflection in the window. "What if that maniac came back and kicked your ass? What is that going to change?"

He walked across the room and flopped down on the couch. His thoughts whirled around in his head. Could he really support himself with an office in this tiny town? There was lots of money in his bank account. No one knew he had it. It would last a long time if he didn't do anything stupid. He doesn't need to practice law. He doesn't need to breathe either, he thought.

As he played out different scenarios of his life, Diane kept rearing her head. Sooner or later someone would find him. Sooner or later, he would have to face the firm and his part as a senior partner. That seemed the least of his worries. But, Diane was vicious. As he ticked off their assets on his fingers, he understood that everything was wrapped up in the firm. The house, his three cars were all assets of the firm.

He tried but he couldn't recall if Diane knew they didn't really own anything. If she didn't and she found out, she would be far worse than the guy in the café. What was he to do? A wave of despair washed over him.

As his thoughts swirled, he drifted off to sleep. He awoke to a different kind of light in the room. He looked at his watch, five-forty-five. There was just enough time to get home for dinner.

His route was always the same, and as the days passed he was beginning to recognize the people along the way. People in their yards, cars passing him with people on their way home from work, the faces were finding their place in his life. He waved occasionally to the shop owners as they began to pull displays and products in from the sidewalk.

"Good evening!" was offered more frequently as Dupree was beginning to be part of something.

The sidewalks ended at the corner of Inspiration Street and Prosperity. The side of the road was uneven and the pavement broken. Dupree was happy to think that the days were getting longer instead of the other way around because he knew the path would be pretty treacherous in the dark.

As he crossed Prosperity at Contentment Street where Grammy's place was, he noticed a dark Camaro that passed earlier. He dismissed it. It's a small town.

The car pulled to the side of the road and turned on its lights. Dupree continued walking but looked back after a few yards.

The sound of the engine revving cut through the cool early evening air. Dupree paid no attention as the engine revved again. He figured the driver was having engine trouble. That was until he heard the screech of the car peeling out. Dupree walked faster; he was still a couple of blocks from home. He certainly didn't want to get hit by some crazy kid in the dimming light.

Behind him, Dupree heard the roaring engine growing closer. He turned to see the car bearing down on him. Dupree froze, not sure what was happening. At the last second Dupree dove into the ditch along the front of an abandoned house. He felt rocks and gravel cut into his legs.

Dupree scrambled to his feet and broke into a run. In front of him, he could see the car screeching and turning around in the street. The near-miss was no accident.

The Camaro's engine roared as the driver revved the engine into a red-line scream. Dupree stopped. What was he to do? The chain-link fence to his right was too high to get over. He looked around frantically for a place to hide. The large dog on his left was already barking out an unfriendly warning.

The time to plan was over. The car's tires burned and blue-black smoke filled the air as it sped toward him. Within seconds the car was upon him. He jumped as high as he could, clawing and clinging to the fence. As the car passed blaring its horn, Dupree caught a frozen image of Travis Slader from the Café, laughing insanely.

Chapter Five

"What's all that racket out there?" Grammy asked as Dupree came through the door.

"Some crazy kid in a hot car."

"What on earth happened to you?"

Dupree looked down at his muddy knees. "I had to jump out of the way."

"Look at your elbows. You're bleeding. Get in the kitchen. I'll clean you up."

Over dinner, Dupree told the story of the car and how he climbed the fence to get out of the way.

"Do you know who he is?" asked Mr. Cooper.

"I didn't get a good look."

"What kind of car was it?" Mr. Perez asked.

"Dark, blue maybe, but its lights were on bright, so I couldn't see inside."

"Now you listen to me. Our little town isn't like that. This is something way out of the ordinary." Grammy was clearly upset by the incident.

"Probably some kids trying to scare somebody, and it happened to be me." Dupree tried to brush off any semblance of an intentional attack. "Too young, too much car."

"All the same, you need to report it to the police." Grammy insisted.

Dupree ignored her suggestion. "This spaghetti is terrific. You guys are really spoiled with food like this."

The two men looked up and smiled.

After dinner, Dupree was invited by Grammy to watch television with her and the other two boarders, but he chose to wash the knees of his jeans in the bathroom sink upstairs instead. In the hall, outside the bathroom, was a small bookcase. In the dim hall light, Dupree chose three books to take to his room.

He lay down on the bed and thumbed through each, deciding on a mystery by an author he never heard of. The copyright date was 1947. Must have missed this one, he thought. Around eight o'clock he nodded off, only to awake after eleven. He changed and went to bed.

Dupree declined the offer of coffee with Grammy the next morning, wanting to get to the Café. As he went through the door the bell tinkled. Overnight someone fixed it. The place went quiet.

"Over here, hero!" Kenny called out. The café erupted in applause.

Head down and embarrassed, Dupree headed for the booth where Kenny sat alone.

"Thanks a lot." Dupree frowned.

"Oh come on, did you really think the story about the man who saved Dara wouldn't get out?"

"TJ?"

"Who else?"

"Dara was the one with the butcher's knife," Dupree chuckled. "Let me ask you something. What's the story with Travis Slader, do you know him?"

Kenny's eyes lost their sparkle, and his expression changed to one of a mix of fear and shame. "I hate him." There was no humor in his words.

"When I was a kid I had some learning problems, you know. Cal was the smart one. Travis was the worst of the bunch when it came to pushing me around. Cal would try and help, but we were small for our age 'cause we were born premature, you know? We had Terry, he was the fighter. He'd jump in and save me from getting beat up. I'm ashamed to admit it, but I was scared to go to school for years. I'd throw up on the way to the bus lot.

"He's a sneaky bastard too. Mean stuff, cruel stuff. One time in eighth grade, he was hiding in the bathroom at lunch. He wouldn't let me use the toilet. He kept pushing me, hitting me in the lower back. I peed my pants. I had to walk across the school to get to the office. Nobody, not one kid, missed that. Travis ran ahead yelling 'Kenny pissed his pants!'

"So you can just imagine what it was like for us having a father who ran a septic tank business. I've heard every poop joke in the world. That's why Cal won't have anything to do with the business."

"Wow. I'm not sure I could have stood it."

Kenny reached down and unbuttoned his shirt sleeves. "I couldn't." He exposed a series of scars across both wrists. "That was junior year of high school. I never went back." Kenny didn't look up for a long moment. "So yeah, I know Travis Slader."

"I'm sorry, if I knew I wouldn't have..."

"No, it's fine, it was a long time ago. But can you believe them making that son of a bitch a sheriff's deputy?"

"He's a cop?" Dupree said in disbelief.

"Sheriff's department, yeah. White Owl is too small for a police department, so it's patrolled by the County Sheriff's Department."

"Why hasn't he been reported?"

"For what? He knows the line, he never crosses it. Do you have family in law enforcement?" Kenny asked.

"No."

"He does. His uncle. If you complain, he gets the complaint. They're all the same. Best thing to do is make sure you never cross him. Especially in uniform."

"This is insane," Dupree exclaimed.

"Welcome to White Owl."

Dupree now understood Dara, saying she would go to the governor. Maybe he only thought he found a nice place to settle.

"What about the Sheriff himself? Can't he be approached about Slader's behavior?"

"It's a big county. He trusts his lieutenant. It's been tried, believe me. It's always his word against whoever, and he's got department backup. We've all learned to just stay out of his way. I suggest you do the same. Head down, mouth shut for a while." Kenny shrugged.

"How's that worked for you?" Dupree asked sympathetically.

"Don't worry, his time will come."

Kenny's word gave Dupree a chill. It was almost prophetic in its utterance.

"Chocolate zucchini?" TJ asked, approaching the table.

"Just coffee today," Dupree replied.

"Alrighty."

"Duty calls. Buck up. It isn't as bad as it seems. He's grown up some since..." Kenny patted his wrist and winked. He left the booth, giving Dupree a pat on the shoulder on his way past.

The cup in front of Dupree turned over and a steaming stream of coffee began to fill it. He didn't look up. Kenny's words still rang in his ears. How could a person like Slader hold a town hostage?

"Don't I get a hello, good morning, nice job on the bell, something?"

Dupree looked up into Dara's lovely smile.

"Good Morning, I..."

"Looks like ol' Travis didn't scare you off." Dara slid into the booth across from Dupree.

"Not yet." Dupree decided not to mention the car incident. "How long has he been harassing you?"

"Since Mitch's funeral," Dara said, turning serious.

"Are you serious? Why haven't you done something? Filed a restraining order, or…" Dupree realized from her expression that he had touched a nerve, "…or used your butcher knife?" He grinned at her.

"I still don't get why the first time someone around here sticks up for me, it is a total stranger."

"I'm not totally strange. I have my moments."

"Don't joke, I'm serious. Couldn't you see how nuts he was?"

"I saw a woman being abused, threatened, intimidated, and I made a decision to intercede. Seeing the crazy came later." Dupree took a sip of coffee. "Dara, something needs to be done. I'm an attorney, let me..."

"No. Let it go." Her tone showed she wanted no more discussion on the subject.

"What's up with you people? First Kenny, now you. You can't let an officer of the law break it at will."

"It would only make matters worse. Let it go."

"You think he'll let it go? You believe that he'll leave you alone?"

"After my tall, dark stranger came to my rescue? Maybe." She gave him a smile that would have melted a glacier.

"Alright. For now. If he continues though, I will take legal action." Dupree didn't smile and his voice lowered. "It's what I do. It works. If you change your mind..."

"That's very kind. But White Owl is my home. I have to get along with even the worst of it."

"Okay." He paused for another sip of coffee. "Good stuff. Say, I finally got to talk to Toby's mother yesterday about being a busboy. She was delighted but has to talk to her husband first. Can you hang on a little longer?"

"Sure, I guess. Yeah, no problem." She stood. "Sometime we'll have to have a real talk. I have a feeling there's a lot to like about you." She didn't smile as she left the booth.

"I'd like that," Dupree said to her back. He finished his coffee, left two dollars on the table, waved goodbye to Dara, and left for his office.

As he approached the building he saw the phone company van pulling up. He made it upstairs several minutes ahead of the phone man. When Dupree grabbed the doorknob, his hand came away covered in a black carbon like powder. He didn't want to think it was the boys who helped with the files, but it was a pretty juvenile stunt. He went to the back door. It was locked and secure. He returned to the office and cleaned off the doorknob. He was pleased to know the boys didn't break in, but he was still curious about the door.

A half-hour later, the office was ready for phone calls and Internet. An hour after that, the UPS man delivered his new laptop. He opened the box and removed the laptop from its packing. He tossed the box aside. It wasn't his L.A. office, but it was all Dupree needed to get started. Pleased with himself, he spun in his chair.

Directly in his line of vision, J. Peter Mitchell, Attorney at Law was beautifully applied to the window in gold foil and black shadow. The font was strong, ornate, and beckoned back in the days when the building was new. The fact it was only about twenty years old didn't take away from the feeling of integrity it gave. Dupree turned back to the desk and began going through the drawers. It only took a moment to find what he was looking for.

He went to the window, took the single-sided razor blade from the desk and began to scrape J. Peter Mitchell from the visual history of White Owl. All that was left was -chell when he heard a soft tapping on his office door.

"Excuse me, but the door was open." A pale woman who carried a few pounds past healthy was standing in the doorway.

"Hello, please come in. What can I do for you?" Dupree shifted to full lawyer mode.

As she approached the chairs in front of the desk, Dupree saw the deep purple bruises along her right jaw. He immediately shifted his gaze to her eyes. Their lovely brown couldn't hide the pain and hurt behind them.

"Please have a seat. My name is Dupree. What's yours?"

"Robin, Robin Epperson."

"Nice to meet you, Robin. Sorry I haven't quite finished decorating. I just moved in." He smiled and tried to convey the safety of his office.

"You're the one who stuck up for Dara, right?"

"I tried to help her, yes."

Robin sat a little straighter. "I need your help. I need to leave my husband." She looked hard to the right. "He did this to me. It's not the first time, either. I've had enough. Can you help me?"

"I believe I can, but I need to ask a few questions. Is that alright?"

"Yes, sir."

"What is your husband's name?" Dupree didn't take notes. He wanted her to feel she was the most important person in the world, not just notes in a file.

"Jeremy."

"And how long have you been married?"

"Six years next month."

"How long has he been hurting you?"

"Always, I mean, since we were dating, I guess." Robin looked down and picked at something on her sweater.

"That's a long time. Does anyone know he is violent?"

"Oh, he isn't violent, really. Sometimes I do stupid things that make him mad. That's when he loses his temper."

"Do you think it's okay for him to lose his temper and hurt you?"

"Course not. It's just that, well sometimes I can be clumsy, or say stupid things."

"If we are going to work together, I need you to understand something from the start. No man has the right to lay a hand on a woman, ever. You are a very pretty young lady and seem very sweet. No one, I mean no one, has the right to hurt you, no matter what you say or do." Dupree paused and took a deep breath. "Look, I have been at this a long time. I have helped the wives of doctors, football players, and movie stars. The one thing they all had in common was some man convinced them that they were too stupid, fat, ugly, clumsy, or a million other things that made it alright for the man to beat them up. It is a lie. Look at me," he said softly. Robin looked up with tears running down her cheeks. "You are not a punching bag. You are valuable. Do you believe me?"

"I guess."

"That isn't good enough. We'll work on it, because it is true."

"Do you have any children?"

"Two, a boy and a girl. Justin is five, and Sissy, Melissa, is two."

"Nice. Now, again, is there anyone who knows Jeremy hurts you?"

"My mom."

"Good, how about the police?"

"That's no use. Travis Slader, the Sheriff's Deputy that you had a run-in with, is a good friend of Jeremy's."

The sound of Slader's name angered Dupree. He waited a moment before continuing. "Robin, do you have anyone away from White Owl you can stay with?"

"My sister lives in Bellevue."

"Could you go stay with her for a few days?"

"Not if Jeremy found out. He wouldn't let me go." Robin suddenly stood up. "I'm sorry. This isn't going to work."

Dupree looked at the terrified woman in front of him and softly said, "Sit down Robin. We can do this. Save you and your children. We have the law on our side. Not the police or Sheriff's Department, but the laws of the State of Washington and the United States of America. Now, who's bigger, Jeremy or the government?"

"You are."

Dupree was taken a bit off guard by her answer, but it gave him even more determination to help her. "Where is he now?"

"In the woods, working."

"That's good. When does he get home?"

"If he stops for beers, about seven-thirty, otherwise, six."

"Do you have a car?"

"Yes." Robin took her seat.

"OK, I want you to go pack for several days. Get the kids and come back here. I'm going to make some calls. Can you do that?"

"He'll kill me if he finds me."

"That's not going to happen. It's going to be fine."

"Are you sure?"

"I am. How long will it take for you to get back here?"

"Thirty minutes."

"I'll be ready."

The moment Robin was out of the office, Dupree started making calls. He knew California; the laws and support services were different, but he knew there must be similar services available even in the back counties of Washington.

After four calls, Dupree was growing more and more frustrated. The pieces just weren't coming together. The fifth call was the most productive. Almost as an afterthought, a clerk at Social Services in Olympia gave him the number of Kirin Winters at the Rural Emergency Women's Center.

It didn't take Dupree long to see Kirin was a no-nonsense advocate who took her job, and the safety and well-being of women, very seriously. He quickly explained Robin's situation, said he would do his work pro bono, and that she was ready to make a break.

Dupree continued. "She urgently needs a safe house. Somewhere her husband can't get to, and if he does, can't get into."

"We have just the place. There are currently eleven women at Serenity House. It has two guards around the clock. I've yet to see anybody get past them."

"This is great. When can we get Robin enrolled?"

"I can be there in an hour," Kirin assured Dupree.

"That would be great. Thank you so much. See you then."

Robin returned in twenty minutes. Her children were frail and showed signs of exposure to verbal and physical abuse in the home. They clung tight to their mother, and as friendly as Dupree tried to be, there was a wall he could not penetrate.

"They don't open up around men much," Robin offered as an apology for the children's rejection.

"Don't give it a thought. A woman named Kirin from the Rural Women's Center will be here in about forty minutes. She is arranging a nice place for you and the kids until we can sort all this out. There is counseling for these guys," Dupree smiled down at the kids; they didn't change expression. "You really need to take advantage of all the services they offer."

"What am I going to owe you? I haven't got any money right now." Robin showed a determination that encouraged Dupree.

"Nothing, let's call this my 'first client freebie.'" He reached in his pocket and took a crisp hundred-dollar bill from the money he planned to open a bank account with. "Here, you're going to need some incidentals. I want you and the kids to be comfortable and not worry about a thing. I got this end."

"I don't know what to say."

"Say you'll find a safe place, and make a new start. These guys need to be in a healthy place where they can begin to heal too."

"I will, I promise." Robin was crying.

"The one thing I know is when you're in an abusive relationship like yours, it always gets worse. You deserve happiness, you remember that. One small detail. I need your signature on a power of attorney. That gives me the right to files and documents on your behalf. I will fax anything that absolutely must have your signature and Kirin will get them back to me." Dupree moved to the desk where he prepared a hand-written document awaiting Robin's signature. "I'm sorry this isn't typed up, but I haven't got a printer yet."

"I really am your first patient."

"That requires a different license," Dupree said with a kind smile. "We'll call you my first client."

"I told you I said stupid things," Robin said sheepishly.

"Not at all! Have you hired a lawyer before?"

"No."

"Well, there you go. I'm flattered you think I'm as smart as a doctor. I'll tell you something I said once when I was first in law school. I called a judge your majesty instead of your honor!" Dupree chuckled. "You see, we all use the wrong word sometimes. I do it a lot."

"Yeah, but you're not stupid."

"And neither are you. Remember this, stupid is doing the same thing over and over when you know better."

"My mom says that's sin."

"Your mom sounds like a smart lady. Do you know the difference between smart people and dumb people? Smart people pay attention to what's going on around them."

"I've always wanted to go back to school. I dropped out. Now, that was stupid!" Robin smiled for the first time.

"You should, and I bet Kirin knows just how you can do it."

"My kids deserve a mom that is educated so they'll see that it is important in life," Robin said, proud of something she believed showed her intelligence.

"I believe you're going to do just that."

"Anybody home?" A voice came from the outer office.

An Asian woman with a ponytail and wearing a well-worn Levi jacket stuck her head in the door of the inner office.

"Kirin?" Dupree asked.

"That's me!" Kirin gave Robin a smile, "You must be Robin. Who are these guys?"

"This is Justin and this is Melissa," Robin said, putting her hands on top of their heads.

Kirin crossed the room and shook hands with Dupree. "I canceled a meeting, so I'm a bit early. Thank you for reaching out. You've done a good thing today." She turned to face the children. "Do they like snacks?" Kirin pulled two small bags of Apple Rings from her pocket and held them out. "Would you like some?"

The children looked up at their mother. "Be sure and say the magic words," Robin said, giving approval.

"T'ank you," Melissa said first.

Justin took the bag and softly said, "Thank you."

"You are both welcome I hope we are going to be good friends. Can you eat those while I talk to mom for a minute?"

"OK," Justin replied.

"Help Sissy get hers open," Robin instructed.

The pair moved a few feet from the children and closer to Dupree's desk.

"You are a brave woman, Robin. I know how hard this is for you because I've been there. We will get you over the hard part. You've got good legal representation here. Mr. Dupree will see that you and the children are protected. My job is to get you to a safe place, get you medical attention as needed, and we have some really great women who have been where you are to show you you're doing the right thing."

"And Jeremy won't know where we are?"

"Not unless you tell him. I think we both know that wouldn't be a good idea."

"I'm not telling," Robin said sharply.

"You're packed for a few days, right? The Rural Emergency Women's Center will provide food and shelter. We'll see what the state and county can do for you, too. All we want you to do is get healthy and find a good, healthy place inside."

"Dupree says you can tell me about going to school?"

"I certainly can. I would be really excited to get you all set up."

"So what's next?" Dupree asked.

"We need to get going. We'll get Robin and the kids all set up and enrolled in the program so we can get services started. I gave you my fax number. Anything you need to be signed just shoot over to me and I'll see they are taken care of."

"Robin, this is all for you. If things feel like they're going too fast or you need to know exactly what is what, you just call time out and we will make sure you know exactly what's going on. Does that sound good?"

"You will do all the divorce papers?" Robin asked Dupree. It was the first time the word was used.

"If that's what you want, I am here for you."

"Do it. Soon as you can. My life starts new today." Robin's eyes showed a fierce new attitude. Dupree knew she would be alright.

"Yes, ma'am, I will fax them to you by tomorrow. Kirin, anything you need from me?"

"This is about the smoothest rescue I've ever done. I feel really good about the future for these guys. Did you drive here?"

"My car is outside."

"Let's do this. Let's transfer your stuff to my van. We'll drop the car back at your house."

"Jeremy's house," Robin interrupted.

"Jeremy's house," Kirin confirmed. "And then we are off. Sound good?"

"Yes, ma'am. Let's do it."

"Thank you, we'll talk later," Kirin said to Dupree. "Come on kids, we're going on an adventure!"

Robin turned and went to where the kids were munching their snack. She knelt down and said something Dupree couldn't hear. She stood and they moved toward the door. Kirin followed.

As they entered the hall, Robin turned and ran back to where Dupree stood and threw her arms around his neck. "God bless you. I'll never forget this." She kissed him on the cheek and ran back out to Kirin and the kids.

"Well, there's a start." Dupree felt a feeling of deep satisfaction for the second time since he left L.A. It was a feeling he liked and he could stand to have more often.

From the window, he watched Kirin move several black garbage bags and the car seats from the back of Robin's car to the van. Justin jumped in the van and said something to his mother. She smiled and gave him thumbs up. Dupree smiled.

Two minutes later Robin's car, and then Kirin's van, rounded the corner at the end of the street.

"You got your first client. Time to get to work!" Dupree said as he went back to setting up his computer. It took a few minutes but Dupree booted it up, connected to the Internet, and logged into his Cloud account. He went right to work finding the documents he would need for Robin.

Olson's should be open by now, he thought, so he closed the door and ran down the stairs to purchase a printer fax machine. As he hit the sidewalk he heard someone calling his name. Up the street, Toby was standing in front of his bench excitedly waving his arms.

"Dupeee! Come here!"

Dupree waved back and started towards the furniture store.

"What's goin' on, buddy?" Dupree called as he crossed the street.

"I'm getting a job!"

"You are?" That wasn't quite according to plan, Dupree thought.

"Yes, yes, yes!"

As Dupree sat down on the bench he said, "Tell me all about it."

"You know. My mom said you ask. My dad got mad. Mom said shut up!" Toby made an angry face, then smiled. "I will pick up dishes. It is called bust boy."

"Busboy," Dupree corrected.

"Bus, yeah, bus. That's what I am."

"You need to talk to Dara at the Café. Did your mom tell you?"

"Yes, no problem. I got this!"

"I'm sure you do." Dupree laughed. "I'm sure you do. Tell your mom to come see me when she gets time. See my window?" Dupree pointed up at his half-scraped window.

"Okay," Toby said proudly.

"I have got to go back to work. Congratulations."

As he left the bench, Dupree could hear Toby behind him singing, "Bust boy, bust boy, I'm a bust boy."

Pete Olson was more than eager to sell Dupree a combination printer, copier, fax machine. It was more than Dupree hoped to spend. Compared to the machines in his office in L.A. it was a toy. Olson assured him it was equipped with all the bells and whistles he would need in a three-way office workhorse, and he did need one and fast. The rest of the money intended for the opening of his bank account was now in Olson's register.

As Dupree opened the box and began to remove the packing material, he realized he had no idea how to set up a copy-printer-fax machine. How hard can it be? he thought. As it turned out, it can be very hard. Just getting the computer to recognize the Wi-Fi signal from the modem, and the printer to recognize the computer, made Dupree swear in exasperation several times.

He was all ready to print a test page when he remembered he threw out all of Mitchell's old discolored paper. He wrote down the fax number provided by the phone company. Quite pleased with himself for remembering the number, he made a return visit to Olson's.

"I need a ream of paper and a favor," Dupree said, entering the store.

"I'm broke," Olson replied.

"Haha!" Dupree offered a sarcastic courtesy laugh. "I need you to send me a fax at this number. I think I have it set up right, but I need to run a test."

"You've had a busy morning. People running in and out," Olson pried.

"First client. Feels good."

"What kind of case?"

"Ah, ah, ah, client confidentiality." Dupree wagged his finger at Olson.

"I heard about you coming to Dara's rescue. Why didn't you shoot that jerk while you were at it?"

"No gun. Besides, I believe that is illegal even in White Owl." Dupree teased.

"Still, you'd probably get a medal. Maybe the girl, too!"

"Why do you people put up with that guy? I mean, it seems everybody hates him. He openly harasses and intimidates people."

"Oh, I don't know. Hometown boy, a few equally rotten friends, an uncle whose nose is permanently stuck to the Sheriff's butt, and people are just afraid enough to not make themselves noticed. Thing is, he knows just how far to go to stay out of any real trouble. I bet you're the first person to stand up to him in ten years."

"Sad deal, for a whole town to walk around on eggshells." Dupree sighed.

"Oh, you know, it runs hot and cold. He'll get a burr under his saddle for a while, gives somebody a hard time, and then he'll lay off." Olson shrugged. "Just don't go rubbing his nose in it. You'll be alright. That's the thing with bullies. They always have a good run, then there's a new bull of the woods. Hell, it could be you!" Olson laughed. "It might be you!"

"Just don't forget the fax. Oh, and put this on my account, would you, Pete?" Dupree said holding up the paper.

"You don't have an account!" Olson protested.

"Start one!" Dupree called from the front door.

"Bully!" Olson yelled back.

The print test worked perfectly the first try. The copy came out perfect. Olson waited almost ten minutes, but finally sent a fax of a "Stop Bullying" sign.

Dupree grinned as he pulled it from the machine.

"Dupree, you now have a functional law office," he said, patting the top of the new machine.

Mission accomplished, he stood and went to the window. Grabbing the razor blade, Dupree went to work finishing the scraping of Mitchell's name off the window. Up the street to his left Dupree saw a sheriff's car coming. It slowed and then stopped in front of Dupree's building. It sat for a minute or more, then backed up and pulled into a parking spot.

Without a doubt, it was Slader. Dupree wasn't about to hide from a bully.

He stepped closer to the window and looked down. At that moment Slader looked up and saw him. His uniformed arm extended full length out of the cruiser's window and he raised his middle finger to Dupree.

Chapter Six

"Is this the Dupree residence?"

"Mom! Phone!" Deanna shrieked. It took several minutes before Diane picked up the phone. "Hello?"

"Diane Dupree?"

"Yes."

"This is Deputy Sheriff Travis Slader. Do you know an Adam Dupree?"

"Yes! He's my husband. Is something wrong?"

"He had a bit of a run-in with one of our locals here, and I ..."

"Where is here?" Diane demanded, all concern gone.

"White Owl, Washington, ma'am. You don't know where he is?" Slader asked.

"No, I mean yes, so what did he do?"

Slader grinned on his end of the line. It was time to set the hook. "We are still gathering the facts, but it seems he and this other fella were fighting over a woman."

Slader paused to let his words sink in. "Anyways, he threatened this fella and well, we may have to press charges. I was calling as a courtesy in case he needed bail." Slader's excuse sounded lame even to him, but the effect wasn't what he expected.

"If I may ask," Diane began, "how did you know his first name was Adam if you haven't arrested him? He never uses his first name." Diane alerted to the odd content of the call.

"Oh, we took fingerprints off his office doorknob."

"His office?"

"Yes, ma'am, he's a lawyer, right?" Slader was delighted at the can of worms he opened.

"How did you fingerprint his office if you're in Washington?"

"The office here in White Owl ma'am. He has another?"

"Who did you say this was?" Diane was now on full alert.

The line went dead. Diane racked her brain, trying to remember what the caller said his name was. Deputy Adam, no that wasn't it, she thought.

"Dammit!" Diane shouted as she slammed down the phone. "Redial!"

She picked up the phone and hit buttons. She heard voices.

"Eric, hang up!"

"Hold on. My cell phone's been canceled. I have to call the company."

"Hang up I said!" Diane started hitting redial. Eric was off the line but she couldn't get a dial tone.

After about thirty seconds she heard the dial tone. She hit redial.

"Pacific Cellular, may I help you?"

"Arrggghhhh!" Diane screamed and slammed the phone down.

Then it hit her. She couldn't redial. That slimeball had called her! Wasn't there some kind of trick for finding out the number of someone who called you? "Oh yeah."

She yelled for her son again. "Eric, what the hell is that number you dial when you want to call back the person who just called?"

"Star-six-nine. But if he's smart he'll have the number blocked. "

Diane picked up the house phone and dialed *69. Sure enough, blocked number. "Arrggghhhh!" Diane growled and slammed the phone down.

It didn't take long networking her divorced friends to find a divorce attorney. Her first appointment went well with her new attorney, L. Simon Sweeney, and her demands were simple: she wanted her half, now! In the time Dupree was gone, she realized how much she enjoyed not having him around. So, after the call from Slader, it only took moments until she was on the phone with Sweeney.

"Good Morning, Diane, how may I make your day brighter?" Raised to the right temperature, Sweeney's sugary approach would make candy.

"I found him, Mr. Sweeney."

"Please dear, Simon."

"He is in some town in Washington State."

"Well, aren't you the little Nancy Drew?" Sweeney gushed.

"So now we can serve him, right?" Diane responded, totally devoid of niceties or any effort to respond to Sweeney's pithy comments.

"We most assuredly can and will. What is the name of the town?" Sweeney realized he was wasting his charm on Diane.

"White Owl."

"Like the cigar?"

"I wouldn't know. How long will it take?"

"I can fax all necessary documents to a process server immediately. How long it takes to serve the papers will depend on locating Mr. Dupree."

"I told you where he is!" Diane wanted results instantly. "I want them served today. I want this filed, over and done with."

"I will put a rush on the serving. I must tell you though, my dear, it will double the servers fee."

"I don't care. Do it." Diane demanded. "Anything else?"

"I will call you when we have proof of the serve. The timing of the return of documents depends entirely on your husband. Once served, it is out of our hands. You do understand that? If Mr. Dupree should choose to not sign, or wait, it is his prerogative." Sweeney was growing tired of his foul-tempered client.

"He can't sign until he has them. I will be expecting your call later today," Diane said, hanging up the phone.

"Yes, yes, yes!" She did a little dance, and chanted to her own tune, as she pumped her fists in the air.

Grammy Morrow invited Dupree for a breakfast of buttermilk pancakes and Loganberry jam. It was an offer he readily accepted. He was not disappointed, and when she offered seconds he happily agreed. Her coffee was a lot better than the café and he loved hearing her stories of growing old in White Owl.

She was full of surprises and then three cups of coffee later when Dupree stood to leave, she presented him with a sack lunch.

"A little something to get you through the day."

"Do all your boarders get this treatment?" Dupree smiled. The sack was as heavy as if there was a brick inside.

"Only the ones I might need to get me out of jail." The old lady winked.

"Well, it's a crime more people can't taste that jam," Dupree said, making his way to the door.

"Smoothie," Grammy said with a sly smile, but Dupree missed it.

Since his first encounter with Travis Slader, Dupree kept a notepad with times, locations, and the facts of his contact with the Deputy. There is a significant difference between the actions of a law enforcement officer on and off duty. The only on duty episode with Slader was the day before when he flipped him off. Try as he may, Dupree couldn't shake the feeling there was more to come.

The morning passed quickly. Two wrong numbers, a survey from the telephone company regarding their service, and a call from Kirin Winters.

"Good morning. I just wanted to give you an update on Robin," Kirin began. "She is a very strong woman, nothing like what I expected. It's refreshing. How are the divorce papers coming?"

"I just printed out the preliminary set this morning. I've been shopping around for a process server."

"What about the Sheriff's Department?" Kirin asked.

"The Deputy that is assigned to patrol in White Owl is a friend of Jeremy's and has ignored complaints in the past. He's no particular fan of mine either. Besides, I want to find someone I can work with from now on. The second I find someone, he will be served, I assure you."

"Great, I'll let her know. And the restraining order?"

"I decided not to file until papers are served. I don't want to tip our hand too early."

"Good call. Let's see, the kid's love the preschool here, so that helps. I think I have a scholarship lined up at Edmonds Community College that should be far enough away to keep Jeremy out of her hair. She's really quite bright. She passed all the GED pre-tests on the first try. She's just been in a bubble for so long, you know. Luckily she likes to read, that always helps. She's going to be okay. Thank you for taking an interest in her. You did a good thing."

"I appreciate the follow-up. Give her my best and tell her I've got this end. I'll be in touch."

"Talk to you later then!" Kirin said cheerfully.

There was a knock on the outside door followed by, "Anybody home?"

"In here!" Dupree called.

A sad-faced man of no more than five foot four, that reminded Dupree of Ringo Starr, came as far as the office door.

"Have a seat," Dupree offered, extending his hand. The man ignored Dupree's handshake and sat down. "What can I do for you?"

"Nothin'. I think you need me. I do process serving around here. I heard you needed somebody. I'm the one you want. I know the territory. I carry both a 9mm automatic, licensed of course and a Taser. I have never had anybody who I couldn't serve. I got a nose like a bloodhound. What have you got for me?"

"That is quite a resume, Mister!" Dupree said, trying to hide his amusement at the business practices of this terribly serious little man.

"Marsh Peterson. It's all true. Don't let my size fool you. I got a, Whaddaya call it, Bonaparte Syndrome."

"Napoleon?"

"That's the one! Used to get me in all kinds of trouble in school." Marsh nodded repeatedly.

"I can see how it might. So what is your standard fee?"

"First one's free, so's the last. Last, meaning if I don't get along with you. First, if you don't get along with me. Fair?" Marsh said, flatly.

"Sounds fair to me. I've got a job ready to go. Jeremy Epperson, know him?"

"Not really. Know of him. Logger, right? Friend of that asshole deputy?"

"That's the one. Pretty simple divorce filing. I will have a restraining order later today."

"Need me to file that?" Marsh asked.

"Yeah, that would be great."

"Have it ready when I come back. Twenty bucks."

"Alright." Dupree was surprised at how cheap Marsh worked. "That will work."

"Might take me a while, I'll have to drive up into the woods. Be back before three. That okay?"

"Fine, what's your cell number?"

"Don't have one. I'll check in once a day. That work?"

"Sure. You want my number?"

"Why?"

"I don't know," Dupree struggled to keep from laughing. This was going to be the oddest of relationships. There was something about Marsh that he liked. "I guess you don't."

"Keeps things simple. I'm a simple man, with simple habits." Marsh gave Dupree a smile that flashed across his lips so fast he nearly missed it.

"I think we'll get along just fine." Dupree gave his new process server a big smile. It was not returned.

Five minutes later Marsh Peterson was out the door and on his first serve. Dupree checked his watch, eleven-thirty.

The concept of practicing law without staff and a client base was completely foreign to Dupree. His first office at least had a secretary, and then he was hired by the firm where he spent his entire career. On his first day at Atherton, Miller, and Chase there were thirty-four case files on his desk. That load only grew. He never needed to drum up business or worry where his next case would come from. The firm was old and established, with more than five hundred clients on retainer. By the time Dupree made partner, that number increased fivefold.

Sitting facing unfamiliar walls, with a clear desk and no secretary, no calls to answer or return, and no network of colleagues to draw from, Dupree wondered what he was to do next. It will take time, he told himself, and time was something he had plenty of.

"Time is a billable commodity." That was his mantra for over twenty years. Time took precedence over family, friends, relationships, and recreation. Multi-tasking to Dupree meant multi-billing, and he was the master. He billed for driving time to and from the office to appointments, and he billed other clients he called from the car. Golf games were billed, so were dinners with clients. Doubling up with another client was manipulated by Dupree in the name of networking for the two, sometimes three, clients. The time was billed.

Sitting idle was new to Dupree. He was beginning to like it. Several times he caught himself sighing deeply. It was as if his soul was exhaling. Years of pressure and stress were lifting from his spirit. Problems and opportunities were looked at in a whole new way. The lack of pressure to do things enabled Dupree to consider more humane approaches to dealing with people. His volatile temper had yet to show its ugly, venomous head in White Owl, and he even took his first case for free. Yes, he was changing.

Dupree waited for Karen Wharton to make an appearance, but she never showed. He refrained from paying her a visit for fear of appearing pushy. He went to the window and there was no sign of Toby. His bench was empty.

"Anybody home?" Marsh Peterson called from the outer office.

"Still here," Dupree said, taking his feet down from his desk.

The only things missing were a sideways hat and his hand in his shirt to make Marsh a perfect Napoleon. He strolled into the office like he owned the place.

"Served. He didn't like it one bit. I was about to Taser his ass when he suddenly calmed down, asked me for a pen, signed the papers on the hood of a truck, and handed them back. That's a home run. That doesn't happen very often, no sir." He thrust out a manila envelope at Dupree.

"That's terrific!" Dupree exclaimed, taking the envelope.

"Yeah, well, that's the good news," Marsh said, almost apologetically.

"There's bad news?"

"Well, for you. Not me. Here's the thing. I don't make a lot of money doing this, you know? I get by, and I've got no complaints, but I always run out of money before I run out of month. So when somebody offers me five hundred bucks for one serve I gotta take it."

"What are you saying?"

"I'm saying I hope we will still be working together after today." Marsh looked down at the floor.

"Because?" Dupree pressed.

"Because you've been served!" Marsh thrust out another envelope.

"You're serving me?"

"'Fraid so. I got the fax just before I left for the woods. Priorities, you understand. Always follow the last order first."

"That is very noble. I'm just amazed I am getting served. Nobody knows I'm here," Dupree said in astonishment.

"Seems somebody does."

Dupree slipped several sheets of white paper from the envelope. "Well, what do you know?"

"I'd say 'What is it?' but I already know. Kinda sucks." Marsh grimaced. "So am I still working for you?"

"Yeah, I have another job for you right now. Two actually."

"I think we're gonna get along."

Dupree didn't respond to Marsh. He reached in his desk drawer, took out a pen, and began drawing lines through items on the document.

"You ever been married, Marsh?"

"Three times. Once for love, once for big tits, and once for money. Love is fickle, tits sag, and well, money runs out, and so did she. Never again, no sir, never again."

Dupree wrote feverishly on the documents. He flipped sheets over several times and wrote on the backs.

"I only did it once. I married for prestige and the image of what I thought a lawyer needed to succeed."

"Didn't work."

"No, it didn't. But you know, this is better than I could have dreamed. I didn't initiate it. I'm not fighting it, and I feel really good. Is that bad? I mean, you're the expert here," Dupree grinned at Marsh.

"You makin' fun of me?"

"Not at all, just looking to the voice of experience." Dupree was making fun a little, but only because he liked the way his new friend spoke.

"The way I look at it, if you're happy she dumped ya, then you win. If it was heartache and alcohol, I'd say you lose. Me, I was two out of three. Only marry for love. She decided she didn't love me anymore, but she left and I was heart broke, for a while, but #2 came along with something different and I said, 'What the hell,' and went for it. I took off on that one. Then ol' money bags, I was real glad to get rid of. Overall, love is for the young. If you do it again, do it for a best friend. I never had one of those and I think I shoulda."

"You are more than the sum of your parts. A wise man indeed." Dupree signed the papers in front of him with a flourish and in several places. "Done, and done."

He slipped the papers back in the envelope. On the other side, he wrote a fax number.

"This one, as is, to this number." Dupree handed Robin's paperwork to Marsh. "This one will need front and back of most of them. I have written page numbers nice and big at the top right of each page."

"Got it." Marsh nodded.

"Oh, and include a note to my wife's lawyer saying, oh, I don't know, something about a difficult serve, and how you insisted on an immediate return. Then tell him the fee is a thousand bucks. They'll pay, guaranteed."

"I never seen a lawyer like you before. I know we're going to get along fine."

"I think so, too. Get me back the papers and an invoice as soon as you can so we can settle up."

"No need, this is what I call pro boner. A freebie."

Dupree laughed heartily. "I never imagined getting a divorce could be so much fun or I would have done it years ago!"

"It's all about the timing. Believe you me, timing is everything." Marsh slapped his thigh with the envelopes and left the office.

The silence of the office seemed to swirl around Dupree's entire being. His life just exploded, imploded, took flight, and crashed. He was a mix of elation and despair. The world he woke to every day for year upon year, in less than a raindrop of ink, was gone. The house he lived in, the car he drove, would be surrendered to the firm. His possessions in the house, most of which he could barely recall, were no doubt in the trashcan by now. The things he most cherished were in his office. Martin Hutchinson would assure they were stored safely. Perhaps tomorrow he will call Martin.

It was unfinished business, loose ends that needed to be dealt with and then forgotten. He felt no nostalgia for the firm. If he didn't think about the list of things he needed to do, the people, office, and work that was his life just a few days ago never entered his mind. The river of time took him farther from guilt, interest, and concern for that life every day. So many thoughts and emotions flooded his soul that perhaps breaking free of that life was something long overdue.

But what of the children, some may say? They were not connected to him in an emotional way. Diane made sure she was the favorite; he was the ogre, the absent being in the house. Even as small children, when he attempted to cuddle, or to show affection or interest in them and their activities, they pulled away from him in favor of her. He could never be accused of indifference or abuse; mental, physical, psychological, or any other kind. He was the victim of systematic irrelevance, though he would never speak those words aloud. He would never speak either of the times he lay in bed and wept at the state of his family relationships. That, more than anything, was the source of his hatred of Diane.

Dupree actually jumped when the phone rang. He was so deep in thought and feelings he was no longer in the realm of the present, but completely submerged in the purging of all unpleasant memories.

"Hi. It's Dara." She paused. "I bet if I asked 'am I interrupting anything', you would think me presumptuous."

"Actually, I was trying to define who I was."

"Heavy. Say, your boy Toby, that's not right, he's twenty-four. Anyway, he came by with his mom. We had a nice chat. I showed him what he would be doing. I asked a lot of questions, and I think it just might work."

"That's great. I was curious about what was going on. I asked that they talk to me before going to see you. You can see how much my opinion is worth." Dupree chuckled.

"Actually, Toby repeatedly, and you know I truly mean repeatedly, said 'Duppee said I could be a Bust Boy.'"

"You really think he can do it?"

"I hope so. It would be nice. So what is it lawyers do in an office all day on what, the fourth day you're open for business?"

"Truthfully?"

"Yes." Dara's sincerity surprised Dupree.

"I was served divorce papers today. Which is pretty strange, since I didn't think anyone outside of White Owl knew I was here."

"How do you feel about that? I'm sorry, none of my business. Are you alright I mean? I don't know what I mean." Dara went silent.

"I'm good. People say this a lot, but it's true, I've had no marriage for nearly twenty years. It is actually a relief that she pulled the plug. Life support was just keeping a dead thing breathing."

"So when you said you were trying to define who you were, that wasn't meant to be funny."

"Not at all. Everything I have known for more than twenty-five years sort of disappeared like a wisp of smoke. So, I was sitting here trying to figure out who I was. Not in some psycho-babble-hippie-guru kind of way, but when you strip away the country club wife, the big house, the fancy cars, and the spoiled kids, and prestigious law firm, who am I?" Dupree took a deep breath. Why am I telling her this? I don't know her and I'm baring my soul to her like she's my priest or shrink or worse, Dupree thought. He was in a panic. He wanted to hang up. He didn't want to talk anymore, but he desperately wanted to hear her voice.

It was silly to have turned a courtesy call into an exposé on his private life. What must she think? His thoughts bounced around in his head like a pinball machine without the flashing lights and dinging. He was a stranger, not a friend, barely an acquaintance, a guy who stood up to a bully and meddled in her employment practices.

"Still there?" Dara asked softly.

"I am."

"When I lost Mitch, I had no one. I mean, we were so close, we didn't really have friends because we wanted to spend every second we had together. Cathy and Carl were great, but they were my in-laws. I desperately wanted to sit in the dark and talk to someone who wouldn't judge me, who would just, be, you know. I didn't even want them to answer or comment or say nice things.

"Your situation is quite different than mine, but I get it. Everything that was isn't. Everything solid under your feet has turned to water. But, what you said, about who am I? That's what saved me. When I took away my best friend, confidant, lover, pal, and was stripped naked of a future with him, who was I?"

Dupree so wanted to say something but he was afraid she would stop talking.

"I found out I didn't like a lot of stuff about me. I realized that part of my love was made up of fear, selfishness, and need. I found out I had to stand up, grow up and see what I could do in the world. Without support, without someone to go home and complain to, cry to, get mad at and just find my way alone. I missed Mitch to the marrow of my bones, I still do at times, but death isn't painful for the dead. So, why do we torture ourselves? They aren't coming back. They don't know we are suffering, it does them no good. So why do it? Is that terrible?"

"No. I believe that, in a way, my life never began. So I can almost feel what you are talking about."

"I have never told anyone the way I feel. In fifteen years, I have never had a conversation that exposed the raw nerve endings I was covered with. I don't know why I feel so comfortable with you knowing." Dara gave a nervous giggle.

"Attorney-client privilege?"

"Please don't make fun of it," Dara pleaded.

"Never. I make dumb comments when I'm nervous. I worked with a fellow for years that could defuse any situation with a clever comment. I tried to emulate him, but my comments always came out wrong. They sound great in my head, but in the light of day, they always fail. I'm sorry."

"Boy, are we damaged. I wasn't being mean; I just needed you to know how much it meant for me to share myself with someone again." It was Dara's turn to chuckle.

"Maybe it is the anonymity of the phone. I don't think I could have said what I did if you were sitting in front of me."

"Why?"

"I don't know, we barely know each other. You're the Queen Bee of White Owl and I'm a runaway." Dupree couldn't help himself. He laughed. "Sorry, I don't know why that struck me funny. This is a wonderful conversation. I don't want to sound like a me-too, but I haven't talked like this to anyone since my mother died."

"You were close?"

"I could tell her anything. She always knew what to say, to make me feel like I mattered. I think I broke her heart when I got married. I think she saw right through it."

"How do you mean?"

"I married Diane because she was beautiful, quick-witted, a social climber, and just what I imagined a lawyer's wife to be."

"Did you love her?"

"Truthfully? I don't think I ever did. I loved the idea of her. So it is entirely my fault, really. The funny thing is I bet she is more relieved than me."

"You said you have children?" Dara asked, hesitantly.

"That's for another day."

"Oh, do you need to hang up?"

"No, no I just want to have a few more days of you thinking I might be alright."

"What does that mean?" Dara asked sharply.

"I don't like them. They hate me. They have been molded in the image of their mother, and they won't miss a beat going on with their self-centered, shallow, selfish lives. See, it sounds pretty horrible."

"Actually, it sounds very matter of fact. I don't sense any anger, resentment, hate, or anything but a lawyer's facts-only statement."

"Ouch!"

"I only want to know one thing. How does it make you feel?"

"Blank, hollow, empty, void of any feeling at all, really. All my tears were shed years ago."

"Wow. I am so sorry. Not for you, for them. They're the losers. I think they've missed out on someone very special." Dara cleared her throat. "That didn't come out right. I mean, special as in the relationship they could have had..."

"Not me?" Dupree interrupted.

"Ugh, lawyers! Always a twisted answer for everything."

Dupree broke into laughter. "You know, you are a piece of work. Say what you mean, and just let it go at that. My new rule. I will take the compliment however it was meant, and cherish it. Special me or not."

"Thank you. And with that, I think I will say good-bye."

"How about, see you later instead? I heard that in a movie. I always liked it. Good-bye is too final. I hope we can talk like this again. I think it would be good for both of us."

"I would like that. Bye."

Before Dupree could say anything more the line went dead.

"Man," Dupree said as he put the phone down. "What a day."

Dupree spun in his chair and looked out the window. A large hawk, or some other kind of large bird, he wasn't sure, was soaring free in the sky above the building across the street.

"And now I'm getting signs from above!" Dupree continued watching until the bird disappeared from view. "Thanks, my friend."

When Dupree looked down, the yellow pad in front of him was nearly filled with notes, projects, and ideas for the new practice. Almost without realizing it, he ate the huge meatloaf sandwich and cookie Grammy packed for him. Never noticing the time, the shadows in the office were showing the signs of the late afternoon sun. Fixed on his work, he didn't notice the sound of the door opening in the outer office.

"Want to tell me who you think you are?"

Dupree looked up to see a man dressed in jeans and an untucked flannel shirt standing in his office.

"Excuse me?"

"I don't stutter. Who the hell you think you are interfering in my family?"

"For starters," Dupree scowled, "who are you, and what gives you the right to barge into my office without knocking, and start yelling? You want to go out and try it again?"

"No, I won't go out again! I'm Jeremy Epperson, and your name is on the divorce papers that troll brought out to my job site. He embarrassed the hell out of me in front of the guys I work with."

"As you said, I did not serve the papers, my associate Mr. Peterson did. Yes, my name is on the documents you signed, because your wife chose me to be her legal representation in her divorce procedures. I apologize if Mr. Peterson was insensitive to your situation at work. However, serving papers of any kind is a difficult process at best, and he has to catch as catch can. Anything else?" Dupree was not pleased with the appearance of the angry spouse. He picked up his pen and wrote, lock outer door, on his page of notes.

"Look, mister fancy pants lawyer, we don't want or need you in our town. We get along without troublemakers like you just fine."

"We?"

"Travis told me how you interfered with his private conversation with his fiancé. Now you're having Robin divorce me. You're a bit too friendly with the women around here. It's time for you to leave." Jeremy was huffing with anger.

"It seems you also get along without law and order. Mrs. Walker has no interest in your friend the deputy and has, according to her, told him so repeatedly. So he is most assuredly not her fiancé. Strange behavior, a law enforcement officer pressing himself on a woman who isn't interested, wouldn't you say? And your wife came to me for help."

"You don't get it. We don't want you in our town."

"We, meaning you and the deputy," Dupree reinforced.

"That's right."

"My turn. This is my office, you are not a client, and therefore not welcome. You need to leave. Your behavior is not, will not, help your case in the divorce proceedings. Threatening or intimidating legal counsel is a felony. There is law outside of White Owl, Jeremy, and it would be quite simple to contact them, taking your friend Mr. Slader out of the loop. I hope you get my meaning. Good-bye, Mr. Epperson."

"Don't talk to me like I'm some kind of idiot!" Jeremy yelled.

"Then don't act like one. Go." Dupree's voice rose for the first time.

Jeremy moved quickly toward the desk and took a wild swing at the laptop. Instead of sweeping it off the desk, as was his intention, his hand hit the side of the monitor, snapping the computer shut.

Dupree jumped to his feet. "I have had enough of you! Get out!" Dupree shouted.

Without a breath of hesitation, Jeremy reached across and grabbed Dupree in an effort to pull him over the desk. Failing that, he began to punch Dupree in the head and neck. The blows were awkward and, for the most part, ineffective.

Realizing what was happening, Dupree threw several punches to Jeremy's ribs. In an effort to release himself from the lock, Jeremy held on his shirt. Dupree rolled to the left. Fabric tore and he landed hard on the floor.

As he scrambled to his feet, Jeremy kicked Dupree in the side, returning him to the floor. Dupree grabbed for Jeremy's ankle in hopes of toppling him but missed. The younger man's advantage of strength and experience was a huge disadvantage to Dupree.

"What in the holy hell is going on!" a familiar voice called from the door.

"Mind your own business, Hobbit!" Jeremy yelled back, kicking a glancing blow to Dupree's shoulder.

Dupree rolled away from the kicks and Jeremy followed. Again trying to get to his feet, Dupree saw Jeremy's feet fly into the air and heard the heavy thud of him landing on the floor. Struggling but standing, he saw Marsh Peterson straddling Jeremy and punching him repeatedly in the face.

"Call me a hobbit, you piece of shit, I'll kick your white trash lumber jack ass from here to China!" Marsh continued punching, landing the best part of his blows to Jeremy's face and forearms as he tried to protect himself from the onslaught.

"Marsh! Enough!" Dupree shouted. "Enough!"

Dupree's words went unheeded and Marsh continued to punch the now helpless young man on the floor. Dupree moved to Marsh and pushed him.

"Enough!" Dupree pushed the little man again.

The blows stopped. Marsh Peterson stood and looked down at where Jeremy lay heaving for breath. "Hobbit my ass!" He shouted down at his motionless foe.

"I'm calling the State Police," Dupree said breathlessly.

"Don't bother. A good beating is what these guys understand. Leave it go." Marsh gave Jeremy a tap with his boot on the side of his head. "You ain't dead. Get up and get out of here. Next time I'll let him call the real cops, not your bullshit deputy buddy. Now get out."

"What kind of a place is this?" Dupree puffed. "I feel like I've come to Dodge City."

"Then you better clean 'er up, Destry." Marsh laughed and tapped Jeremy on the side of the head again. "I said get up."

Chapter Seven

"It would appear you have a broken rib, and a couple badly bruised."

"And?" Dupree asked.

"And they are going to hurt until they heal. Well, I got you wrapped up good and tight. I got some samples of pain pills I'll give you, but other than that, you seem to be okay. Who set your nose?"

"A friend in California. Why?"

"Good job."

"So what do I owe you?"

"Nothing. It will be worth it to see Jeremy Epperson come in here to get looked at. I delivered him, you know. I should have done an abortion." The old doctor gave a phlegmy cough. "Travis Slader, too. What a couple of..."

"And nobody does anything," Dupree said with disgust.

"Ol' Marsh just did. If I were him I'd go on a cruise to the South Seas though. They'll come back looking for blood." The doctor reached in a drawer in the side cabinet. "You care for?" he asked, tipping the flask towards Dupree. "I do, it's medicinal. I write my own prescription." The doctor burst into a mix of coughing and laughter.

"People are basically sheep, Mr. Dupree. They'll let the wolves pick 'em off until there's none left. Some people left, some just stay out of the way. God, I hate this place."

Dupree winced and slid from the examination table. "Why do you stay?"

"Who else would come here to open a practice?"

"The same kind of person that would come here to open a law office," Dupree offered.

"Maybe so, maybe so." The doctor took another sip from his flask. "Maybe so."

By the time Dupree finished with the doctor, it was nearly five-thirty. He headed for home. All along the way, he kept looking over his shoulder. Several times he thought he saw the black Camaro.

As he walked, the thought of packing up and moving on turned and tumbled in his mind. L.A. wasn't as crazy as this place, he thought, or was I just shielded? There was a doorman, a security guard in the lobby, a receptionist at the office entrance, his personal secretary, and big heavy doors between him and anyone who didn't have an appointment or was the least bit threatening. Is White Owl how things are in the real world? A world outside the multi-million-dollar bubble I worked in? He walked on.

There are two, maybe more, men that the town hates. They think they have some privilege of birth, native sons. Strangers threaten their world. I have come and shaken it to its core. I should leave, he thought, I owe these people nothing. They probably wouldn't even notice.

Then ahead of him in the fading light, on the curtain of his thoughts, he saw Dara. Her smile loomed in the curve of the street, her white forelock seemed to light his path. He knew beautiful women, he saw beautiful women every day, at work, on the street, yet none played upon his thoughts and mind like Dara.

What was it about this simple, small-town café owner that was so different? When they talked earlier, even her voice seemed to reach inside and say, it's alright, we got this. She knew him. That's stupid, he thought. They just met, they spoke for no more than ten minutes altogether, yet she reached out to him. Was it just gratitude for interceding with Slader?

What was he to do about her? This wasn't a romantic infatuation. He liked her. She touched somewhere in his soul. I haven't even thought of her as a lover. I just want to sit and talk to her. What is this feeling, he asked himself?

A truck drove past, refocusing his thoughts. He looked right and left and didn't recognize the houses. Turning, he saw the rooster atop Grammy's mailbox. He was so deep in thought he walked right past.

"OK. This has to stop," Dupree said aloud, as he turned and started back toward home.

He glanced at his watch as he opened the front door. Five minutes to six. Just enough time to wash up, change his shirt and get down to dinner.

"My Lord in heaven, what is it now!" Grammy exclaimed as Dupree closed the door. "Just look at that shirt! What is this?" She approached and pulled back his torn shirt, revealing the bandages. "What has happened now?"

"The husband of a client took exception to my representing his wife in divorce proceedings," Dupree said, smiling down at the old lady.

"I didn't realize that lawyering was a contact sport."

"I guess the rules are different around here."

"You feel like eating? Chicken and dumplings tonight."

"That might be just the thing. I think I may join you for some TV later too if you don't mind."

"That would be fun! CSI is on."

"I'm in." Dupree didn't have any idea what she was talking about. He just didn't want to be alone.

"Hey, you alive in there?"

There was a pounding somewhere and someone yelling, but Dupree couldn't figure out where it was coming from. He opened an eye. The room was light.

"Are you alright? Mr. Dupree?" Grammy's voice came through the door where she stood knocking.

"Just a minute," Dupree answered from a fog, unable to understand why she was calling him.

He rolled over and stood. The room spun and he sat back down. Why am I still dressed? His thoughts were a blur.

"You better come in," he said in a voice that seemed far away.

The old woman slowly opened the door. "You alright?"

"What's wrong?"

"It's eleven o'clock. I was worried."

"It must be the pain pill I took."

"You went to bed at nine. Said you were hurting."

"At least I don't have to get dressed," Dupree said, getting to his feet.

"I think coffee is in order."

"Please."

"I'll see you downstairs," Grammy said, leaving the room.

Dupree glanced over at the dresser where the box of pain pills set. He grabbed the box and tossed it into the wastebasket on his way to the bathroom. By eleven-thirty, he was on his way to his office. The coffee helped partially clear his head. He counted on the fresh air to do the rest.

The pain in his ribs was like a dull punch, reminding him with every step they were angry at being kicked. The light of nearing noon was obscured by a thin cloud cover that seemed to move across the sky like it was in time-lapse photography. As he walked, he thought of the events of the previous day and tried to remember if he thanked Marsh adequately for saving him from what could have been a devastating beating. The pain in his side could have been much worse, and hospitalization was a very real possibility. He must thank Marsh the next time he sees him.

As he walked he felt he was being drawn to The Quarter Moon. He needed to get to his office, he needed to alert Kirin to Jeremy Epperson's attack on him. But then there was that pull of the little café. He was forced to admit it wasn't for food or chocolate zucchini bread, it was Dara.

As he rounded the curve in the road he saw more cars and activity than usual in front of The Quarter Moon. The closer he got, the more concerning it became. The Sheriff's Department cruiser was out front, blue lights flashing. Dupree tried to walk faster, but the pain was too much and he was unable to keep up the pace.

About a hundred yards out, the cause of the excitement was evident. Every window in the front of the building was broken; Some shattered and in place, others blew completely into the building.

A group of men was gathered at the end of the building, unloading sheets of plywood from a pickup. As Dupree approached he saw TJ with a wide push broom pushing broken glass towards a large black trash bin.

"I wondered when you'd show up!" a voice called out.

Dupree scanned the crowd. Standing between two cars he could see Kenny, Cal, and Terry.

"What in the world happened here?" Dupree asked, trying to take in the extent of the damage.

"Somebody shot ball bearings into the windows last night. Wrist Rocket I expect," Terry said.

"A what?" Dupree asked.

"High powered slingshot." Terry made a fist and pretended to pull a pouch back from it.

"Sure did the trick," Cal offered.

"Bastard Slader did it!" Kenny's anger was running hot.

"Cool it. He'll hear you," Cal scolded.

"I don't care. You know it was him."

"I don't know anything of the sort."

"Yeah, whatever," Kenny grumbled.

"What a mess. Dara OK?"

"Haven't seen her. We came by for lunch. Place is locked up."

"Who's with her?"

"I saw Carl and Cathy. And Deputy Dog of course."

"When did he get here?"

"Six."

"Six! How long does it require to take a statement from someone who wasn't here?"

"You tell me, you're the lawyer," Cal complained.

"Ten minutes tops. I'm going in."

"I wouldn't," Terry said to Dupree's back. "Shoot yourself."

The door was locked but Carl looked in his direction when Dupree rattled the handle. Cathy waved a come here gesture, as Carl moved to the door.

"Hell of a mess, huh?" Carl unlocked the door and let Dupree in.

"Nobody was here, right?"

"No, it happened sometime in the middle of the night."

"Why is Slader still here?"

"Biggest crime of the last twenty years. He's got to be right in the big middle of it."

"Hi Cathy, quite a mess!"

"I just can't believe it."

"Is that your camera?" Dupree pointed to a small camera setting on a table.

"Yes. I thought she might need pictures for the insurance company."

"Good thinking. I haven't seen Dara," Dupree said, glancing around.

"She's in the office. Go on back," Cathy said with a sly smile.

Travis Slader came from the kitchen with a big slab of nut bread in his hand. "What the hell you want?" he mumbled at Dupree, still chewing a big bite.

"Legal counsel. Are you about done here?" Dupree was all business.

"What's it to you? If your official investigation is completed, I am asking, on behalf of my client, for you to vacate the premises. You have been told you are not welcome and your presence would be considered trespass."

"I'm here in my capacity as the Deputy Sheriff assigned to White Owl."

"And you've been here since 6:00 a.m. There are no witnesses. You've had more than adequate time to complete what little there is to be done here. As I said, if your inquiry is complete, please leave."

"You are really grating on my nerves. How's the ribs?" Slader swallowed hard and grinned.

Dupree glared at the deputy and tasted his words. Deciding nothing would be served by escalating an already volatile situation, Dupree turned and continued to the office.

He knocked gently on the door.

"Come in."

"How you doin'?"

"Hi! I'm so glad you're here. Have a seat. I'd be a lot better if everybody went home and left me to figure all this out." Dara waved her hands across a desk full of papers.

"Have you found your insurance policy by any chance?"

"Yeah, it's right here, but I can't make heads or tails of it. I've never had to use it."

Dupree reached over and picked up the policy. "How about I handle that for you?"

"Really? Oh, that would be great." Dara was more than a little relieved to have help.

"I also asked the deputy to leave." Dupree looked at Dara and waited for a response before going on.

"How can you do that?" Dara's voice went to a whisper.

"I told him I was your legal counsel, and to vacate the premises if his inquiry was completed. I hope that's alright."

"Alright? I could kiss you!" Dara squealed quietly.

Dupree could feel his face flush. "That won't be necessary. All in a day's work," Dupree quipped, trying to sound unaffected by the best compensation he was ever offered for legal services.

"Is he gone?"

"I don't know. I asked him to leave and then came in here. If he's not, he will be facing a restraining order. Honestly, he's really been here since six?"

"Six-thirtyish, yeah."

"Unacceptable and unnecessary."

"I figured he'd leave once Cathy and Carl got here. We just ignored him."

"Oh, boy." Dupree shook his head. "Does White Owl have a glass company?"

"Phil, our glass guy here in town, doesn't have anything this big in stock. He'll have to order it. It'll be here tomorrow. Some of the regulars volunteered to put up plywood until then."

"I saw them unloading. That's really nice." Dupree felt an uncomfortable silence set in.

"Can I cook you dinner tonight?" Dara asked bluntly. "Is that too forward? I mean we just, I just thought… I like your company. It has a very calming effect on me and I need calming. It is totally selfish."

"Yes." Dupree interrupted. "I would like that very much."

"Oh, good. I was afraid I might…"

"You worry too much." Dupree cut her off again. "We can just relax and have a nice long talk. I am dying for company that is under seventy-five and doesn't want to beat me to death."

"Then it's a date!" Dara said cheerfully.

"What time?"

"Six?"

"My dinner hour. Where will this dinner be served?"

"My house, of course."

"I meant, where do you live?"

"Oh," Dara giggled. "Behind Grammy and down two houses. Go through her back fence and skip through the yard. The house is empty. Nobody will care."

"I guess I'll get to work then. I'm so sorry about the windows."

"We both know who did it, don't we?" Dara asked softly.

"I hope we're wrong."

"But you know we're not."

Dupree stood and looked down at Dara. "I promise you this will end, and end soon."

"I told you I didn't want to get him riled up. It'll never end. It's my fight. Please don't get involved."

"Too late." Dupree lifted his shirt, exposing the wrapping around his ribs.

"My God, who did that to you?" Dara stood.

"Jeremy Epperson. With encouragement from Slader, I'm sure. The good deputy also tried to run me over the other night after our little confrontation. So, I am involved. Now we handle this my way."

Dupree took the doorknob and turned. "I will see you at six with a report from the insurance company."

"Thank you, Dupree. You're very sweet."

Dupree smiled and took in Dara's beautiful smile. "This will all sort itself out, don't worry."

Outside, Dupree walked to the center of the crowd. "Hey, everybody! I just talked to Dara. She is thankful for your concern and appreciates you being here, but she has asked that you please go home or back to work or whatever. She will be leaving as soon as the plywood's up. She'll be back in business in a couple of days. Thanks!"

Starting with the twins and Terry, the crowd began to make their way to their cars.

"Where you goin'?" Terry called out.

"To my office."

"Want a lift?"

"Yes, sir!" Dupree went to the passenger side of Terry's beat-up old pickup.

"One thing's certain." Terry began.

"What's that?" Dupree asked, shoving who knew what from the seat and getting in.

"You ride in this turd hearse, nobody's ever gonna say you're stuck up!" Terry laughed and pulled a half-smoked little cigar out of his pocket and shoved it in his teeth.

It seemed like seconds before the truck pulled up in front of Olson's.

"Stay out of trouble."

"Is that possible around here?" Dupree asked, slamming the truck door.

He didn't hear Terry's response due to the grinding of gears and the rusted-out muffler.

He locked the outer door to his office behind him. Within ten minutes he received an appointment time from a claims adjuster and a guarantee that Dara's deductible would be waived.

Dupree stared at the phone for a long moment before punching in the number on his laptop screen for the Washington State Police. He took a deep breath as the number rang. What kind of Pandora's Box are you opening, he wondered?

"Investigations Division. This is Linda, how may I help you today?"

"Hi Linda, this Adam Dupree. I'm an attorney in White Owl." Dupree tried to sound as chipper and friendly as his hesitation would allow. "I need your help. I need to talk to an investigative detective who's a tough, no-nonsense kind of guy. Know anyone who would fit the bill?"

"Burt Carr. He's as nasty and cantankerous as they come. I love him. Want me to connect you?"

"Sounds like my kind of guy."

"He retires next month, so he is even more Burt than usual. Don't let that fool you though, he is as professional as they come. A real teddy bear down deep. Don't quote me!" Linda laughed. "Hang on."

"Carr."

"Good morning."

"Not anymore, it's one-thirty."

"You are a detective."

"Funny. What do you need?" Carr was not amused.

"My name is Dupree. I'm an attorney in White Owl up north."

"I know White Owl."

"Good, here is my problem. We have a deputy sheriff who is riding roughshod over the law. He bullies, intimidates, and abuses the locals. His uncle is next up the food chain, so complaints stop there. One of his buddies attacked me, broke a couple of ribs. Reporting it would go nowhere because I intervened on behalf of the owner of the local café when I first came to town."

"Quarter Moon?" Carr injected.

"Yes, sir."

"Nice lady. What's his problem with her?"

"He is under the delusion she's his fiancé. I walked in when she was telling him she wanted nothing to do with him, never has, and to get out of the café. It just got worse from there when I tried to help. So, he has it in for me too. Even tried to run me down when he was off duty."

"Why aren't you calling the sheriff?"

"The uncle, who is a lieutenant in the department, and the sheriff, are lifelong friends. Everyone who has tried that line just ends up on the deputy's list. So, I thought I would try State Police in hopes we can use attorney intimidation to get the guy that attacked me. State law, State cops? I represent his wife in her divorce action. His name's Jeremy Epperson. He's a wife-beater. She can't report the abuse because the sole law enforcement officer in White Owl is her husband's best friend."

"Hell of a mess you have there."

"More than one. Somebody shot out all the windows in the café last night."

"You think this deputy had something to do with that?"

"Motivation, means, and opportunity, right? Motivation, she rejected him; means, all these people here seem to have a wrist rocket; and opportunity, who else is out in the middle of the night around here without looking suspicious?

"Sure you're not a cop? So, who exactly is this guy?"

"Deputy Travis Slader grew up here; he's been a bully all his life. People are either scared of him, or scared to get on his bad side."

"Besides getting your ribs kicked in and almost getting run over, what's your stake in this? The girl?"

"Justice."

"Not revenge?"

"I've been a lawyer way too long to know that never works."

"So this beating you took, any witnesses?" Carr asked.

"A process server named Marsh Peterson."

"Officer of the court, good witness."

"One problem. In his efforts to save me he gave Epperson a bit of a pounding."

"Doesn't matter."

"Where'd all this happen?"

"In my office."

"Trespass?"

"Yes, I told him to leave, twice."

"Anything else?"

Dupree paused. "Detective, I've interviewed and cross-examined hundreds of witnesses. Slade was enjoying the damage far too much to not have been involved. His cockiness and sheer arrogance showed his contempt for the owner, Dara Walker. He is involved, I'd bet on it."

"My plate is pretty full today. How about I drive up tomorrow, meet you at your office? Does that old gal, Grammy something, still take in boarders?"

"You do know White Owl! She sure does, I live there myself."

"See if she can put me up, will you? I just might stay a couple of days. I'll see you tomorrow."

"I'm on..."

"I can find you. I'm a detective, remember?"

"No dinner tonight, Grammy," Dupree said, entering the kitchen.

"Sick of my cooking already?"

"No, I have a date," Dupree said proudly.

"Who's the lucky fella?" Grammy giggled at her joke.

"For your information, my good woman, I am dining with Dara Walker this evening."

"How did you finagle that?"

"I didn't, she asked me."

"In my day that just wasn't done, darn it. Imagine the fun I would have had!"

"I don't imagine you had any trouble getting dates. I've seen the pictures in the living room. Hubba, Hubba!" Dupree teased.

"I can still chase you upstairs!" Grammy laughed. "You got a clean shirt?"

"Yeah, I sure wish I could shower. The doctor said not to mess with these bandages for at least three days."

"Oh, what's that old drunk know? You want to get the girl or smell like a lumberjack?"

"I'll freshen up the best I can, and not mess with the bandages."

"I'd be happy to help," Grammy winked.

"I can't have two women fawning over me. You stay put."

"Not your best look," Dupree said, looking in the hall mirror as he prepared to go downstairs.

He slipped out the back door as quietly as he could and made his way across the back yard. There were two fence boards missing in the corner. Dupree regretted not walking around the corner when a sharp pain and muscle spasm hit him as he bent to go through the hole in the fence. He stood and lifted his arms above his head to try to relieve the pain. Across the yard, he spotted a bush with a few flowers that were beginning to bloom as the weather improved. Not having a knife, he snapped the flowers from the bush and made a small bouquet. He carefully took a stem, stripped the leaves, and used it to tie the four flowers together.

In the twilight, he saw a house. It was the only house on the block that could possibly belong to Dara. Like Dorothy opening the door to Oz, her house seemed to be the only one with life to it. The pale-yellow paint lifted it from the rest of the dull greens, tans, and blues. The white trim almost seemed to glow in the fading light. A dozen or more wind-chimes hung from the front porch. Dupree stood at the end of the drive and took in the sight of the warm golden light coming from the front window. As he made his way up the walk he saw a swing in the corner of the porch. Any moment he expected to see Norman Rockwell sitting at an easel painting the scene.

"I couldn't imagine a more perfect house," Dupree said to himself as he stood at the bottom of the three steps leading up to the porch.

He carefully mounted each step to help control the impact on his ribs. The glass window in the front door gave a view of the entry and front room. The house seemed to be laid out much the same as Grammy's, but instead of a feeling of the last century and a woman at the end of her journey, this house seemed to smile with the optimistic promise of the future.

He gave three quick knocks on the front door.

"If that's you, Dupree, come in! Anybody else, go away!" Dara called from inside.

As he took the cold brass handle in his right hand, Dupree heard the sound of a muscle car behind him. He turned to see the black Camaro slowly approaching the front of the house. It stopped at the end of the sidewalk leading up to the steps. The engine revved hard before it continued on. Dupree opened the door and went inside

"In here!" Dara called cheerfully.

Dupree followed the sound of her voice into a large, well-lit kitchen. It was a magical space that spoke of a woman who loved to cook. Pots and pans hung from a rack on the ceiling above a huge butcher-block island.

"I hope you're not hungry, I didn't fix much," Dara said, turning from a large industrial style stove.

She held up a broiler tray with two massive steaks. "You look like a man who could use some beef."

"Wow! No girly food around here!"

"Hey, I resent that! Girls like steak too!" She set the tray on the island and took off her oven gloves.

"They look terrific," Dupree said, moving toward the island.

"Are you practicing to be a bridesmaid?" Dara grinned.

"What? Oh!" Dupree said, realizing he was still holding the flowers. "These are for you."

"How delightful! First flowers of the season. How appropriate. Where'd you steal them?"

Dupree knew he was in the presence of a woman of special qualities, and a wicked sense of humor. She wasn't the least bit shy or unwilling to say whatever she wanted. He got glimpses of her wit in flashes when they spoke in the café and in their phone conversation. Here on her home turf, she was completely relaxed and vibrant in a way he never saw before. Her inner strength and confidence amazed Dupree. This was the woman who hours before was dealing with the aftermath of a vicious attack on her business.

"Where should I put them?"

"Here, give them to me." Dara moved around the island and took the flowers. Without warning, she moved in and kissed Dupree on the cheek. "I love them, thank you, it's very sweet."

There's that word again, Dupree thought, as he tried to overcome his shock at being kissed. He couldn't remember that last time someone said he was sweet.

"Can you get me some glasses over there?" Dara pointed at a cupboard with glass insert doors. "I know you don't drink so I got Coke, Pepsi, sparkling cider, and iced tea." She moved to the mammoth, double-door, stainless steel refrigerator. "The Coke - Pepsi thing is kind of a test." She glanced around inside the fridge. "Let's see, I take you for a Roquefort kind of guy, right?"

"Right, I love it." Dupree couldn't contain his pleasure in watching her scurry about putting their dinner together.

"What am I missing?" Dara asked, glancing across the island. "Oh, jeez, the potatoes!" Dara put on her gloves and opened the oven door. "The works, right?"

"The works?"

"Yeah, salt, pepper, sour cream, butter, bacon bits, chives?"

"No chives. I never could figure out the point of them."

"Good, I forgot to get any! The table's set. Food's ready. You're here. Nothing else required. Mind if we plate up in here?"

"Not a bit." Dupree couldn't figure out if this was her restaurant mode or if she was just this relaxed with him. He hoped for the latter. He was totally at ease. His nervous excitement, which peaked entering the kitchen, was replaced with a genuine ease around this beautiful woman.

"I went medium rare on the steak. Is that OK?"

"Just the way I order it. This is fantastic! Grammy is a good cook, but I have been needing a real meal!" Dupree took the plate offered by Dana.

"This way," she said, leading him from the kitchen.

The dining room was exactly as Dupree would have expected, a dark chair rail and wainscoting. The pale green paint above hosted three simple paintings on different walls. A large antique hutch filled the wall opposite the door, and its finely carved detail was breathtaking.

"That is magnificent!" Dupree exclaimed, entering the room.

"Isn't it majestic? A lady named Grace, who ate breakfast every morning for the first ten years I was open, left it to me in her will. Can you believe it? She said I was the only one who smiled at her all day. Bless her heart, I had no idea."

"What a lovely tribute," Dupree said softly.

"Right or left?" Dara nodded toward the table.

"Right?"

"You win again. Have a seat."

Dupree set his plate on the woven bamboo placemat and sat down. The first thing he noticed was a low, long, twisted arrangement of thin branches and thick braided copper wire.

"Like it?"

"Yes, it is really unique."

"People usually say that when they hate something, but I agree. I never saw anything like it. I paid the kid who made it twenty-five dollars."

"Kid?"

"Yeah, I bought it at the High School Art Show."

"That's even better," Dupree said approvingly.

"I like it because you can see and talk over it." Dara smiled. "This house has something we do before meals. I hope it doesn't make you uncomfortable, but it is part of who I am." Dara closed her eyes and bowed her head. "Heavenly Father, I just come to you tonight with a grateful heart. Thank you for no one being hurt in the window incident. And thank you for my wonderful friends who came to my aid. Thank you for providing us with your love and bounty. I especially want to praise and thank you for sending Dupree into my life at this time. Bless him, show him your love, and heal his heart. In Jesus name we pray, Amen." Dara looked up to see Dupree with his eyes still closed.

"Thank you. I mean this in the best way possible. You pray just like my mom used to. Like God was sitting at the table with us."

"He is."

"I've missed that."

"Let's eat!" Dara gave Dupree her dazzling smile and he could have died a happy man.

The two ate in silence for several minutes, interrupted only by Dupree's mmmm's of approval.

"Tell me something," Dara said, finally breaking the silence. "Why Dupree? I mean you're not Bono or Cher." She giggled. "What is your name? Really, I mean."

"Adam Michael Dupree." Dupree shrugged. "Dupree is part of the attorney mystique, I guess. It started in high school. Other guys called each other by their last names. When I went to college I thought it gave an air of mystery. Silly, huh? In law school, a prof asked me my name in class and I said 'Dupree.' A room full of my peers heard it and it was set. It became my signature, and once I passed the bar I used it with my colleagues and clients. It just stuck, I guess."

"It doesn't seem to fit you. I like Adam. Adam you are. Just when we're alone. I don't want to shatter your image." Dara's eyes seemed to twinkle with mischief.

"My turn."

"Uh oh."

"Tell me about your forelock."

Dara reached up and touched the white streak in her hair. "People say that if you have been touched by a ghost, a spot of your hair turns white. I don't believe in such foolishness." She cleared her throat. "About a week after Mitch's funeral, I woke up one morning and shazam, there it was. Now, I don't believe in ghosts or paranormal visits or any of that stuff. But the kind of intriguing thing is, that spot is where Mitch would bend down and kiss me when he left for work. So, in a way, it is a nice reminder of him. It is not the touch of a ghost, though," she said emphatically.

"I hope that didn't embarrass you or bring up painful memories."

"Not at all. Mitch was a wonderful man. I still miss him, at times a lot. But I believe as he did, that he's in heaven. So someday I will see him again. It really hurt to lose him. They say the pain never goes away, but I've found, as time goes by, I become less and less aware of it."

"Gee, with our two mysteries exposed, what on earth do we have to talk about now?" Dupree chuckled nervously.

"Tell me about the insurance."

For nearly four hours, they talked non-stop. After dinner, they moved to the overstuffed u-shaped leather couch. Dara kicked off her shoes and insisted Dupree do the same. No subject seemed off-limits, from teen acne to their greatest fears. Soul bearing was tempered by first car, favorite color, favorite ice cream, and best movie ever made. Around ten-thirty, Dara yawned.

"Me too. It has been a long day for you. I'm sorry the time just flew by."

"Not me. I have loved every minute of it. We didn't even get to our best Christmases and worst dates!" Dara laughed softly. "I think you are very special."

"I've never been accused of that."

"For someone so smart and powerful in their persona, you have a pretty sad opinion of yourself. I'm going to work on that."

"Are you?"

"Yes, when you take me out to dinner."

"When is that?" Dupree was once again taken off guard by Dara's delightful way to speak the truth.

"I'm open for several days. And nights. How about tomorrow?"

"I would like that very much."

"Oh," Dara said, jumping up from the couch. "I have something for you."

She disappeared into the kitchen and Dupree put on his shoes. He was standing in the middle of the room when she returned.

"I thought you might need a fix," she said, handing him a clear plastic-wrapped loaf of chocolate zucchini cake. "It might be a couple of days 'til The Quarter Moon is up and running."

"Now, that is one thoughtful gift!" Dupree said lightheartedly. He moved to the door. "It has been a wonderful evening. I can't remember the last time I laughed so much or smiled so much. Thank you."

"I have really needed someone I could be me with. I'm talked at, all the time, at the café. It is my personality or something, I guess, but no one ever wants to talk with me. You know?"

"They don't know what they are missing."

"Goodnight, Adam." She went up on her tip-toes and kissed him gently on the lips.

They stood, looking into each other's eyes for a long moment.

"Thank you," she whispered.

"For what?"

"The list is getting too long to tell you. Mostly for just being you."

Dupree reached for the door handle, turned, and gave her one last look. "Good night."

Chapter Eight

The forceful knock on the outer office door demanded attention. When Dupree opened the door, a thick man with a bulbous red nose and deep creases in his face stood before him.

"Dupree?"

"You must be Carr."

The man flashed an ID wallet and badge.

"Come in please," Dupree offered.

"Is this your minimalist period?" Carr asked, looking around the sparse office.

"Something like that. Come on back to my office."

Carr took a seat across the desk from Dupree. "How long you been here?"

"Couple weeks in town, here about four or five days."

"You're quite a guy. I did some checking on you."

"I would be surprised if you didn't," Dupree said, without expression.

"Why would a high-powered L.A. lawyer settle in a spit drop like this?"

"You said it already, it's my minimalist period."

"Seems a lot of people in L.A. are looking for you." Carr's casual tone was changing.

"Not anymore."

"Why's that?" Carr scowled.

"I got served divorce papers. Seems the mystery's over." Dupree smiled. "So nothing much there."

"You didn't commit a crime anybody cares about, so it's none of my business."

"You really aren't here for me. What did you dig up on Slader and Epperson?" Dupree shifted the focus of the conversation.

"Let's see, here's what I got on your two boys. Epperson is on probation, suspended five-year sentence for nearly beating a guy half to death in a bar after a Seahawks game. With your witness's statement, I can violate him and he's off to serve his five years."

"Will his wife need to make a statement?"

"Won't make much difference, he's going away. Unless she wants her pound of flesh and a whole other trial."

"No, I'm sure she doesn't."

"I've already notified Probation. They'll be here sometime before noon."

"And Slader?"

"Now, the deputy is a whole other thing. He has a juvenile record that's sealed. I didn't bother, but I can just imagine after what you told me. There are numerous complaints on file for Mr. Slader, but as you said, they were all swept under the carpet. Everybody from the sheriff on down has got his back.

"Especially his uncle. He's a real a piece of work. WBI had him under surveillance for a year. Corruption, misappropriation of funds, but the sheriff called in a few markers and the file disappeared. It was too expensive to start over so it all was dropped. Why isn't the sheriff voted out?"

"Everybody loves the guy in the rest of the county. He has political aspirations and friends in high places. Slader's uncle is his lifelong friend, drinking buddy, and fixer. Your guy is just a minor annoyance to them. And so long as he doesn't kill anybody, they don't care about White Owl."

"Have you got anything on him?"

"Nope. Our best chance is he slips up, says something incriminating, or references your beating. Otherwise, I'm stumped. Arresting his friend might piss him off enough for him to say something stupid."

"What about Dara Walker?"

"She's next. I assume you are her legal representation?"

"Yes."

"Then you will want to be present. Here or at her home?"

"Let me call her."

"Are you two, you know, involved?"

"Apart from the incident in the café, casual passing remarks, a phone conversation, and dinner last night? No, we are becoming friends. Nothing romantic at this point, if that's what you're asking."

"You know it was." Dupree wondered if the old detective was blushing.

Dupree picked up the phone and punched in Dara's number from a scrap of paper next to the phone. "Good morning," he began. "Thank you again for dinner last night, it was delicious."

"Is someone with you?" Dara sensed stiffness in Dupree's words.

"As a matter of fact, I have Detective Carr from the Washington State Police here with me in my office. He would like to talk to you regarding Deputy Slader. He asked me, as your attorney, if you would like to be interviewed at home or here?"

"You're kind of cute when you are in lawyer mode," Dara teased, knowing Dupree couldn't respond.

"That would be an observation observable by you alone."

"And clever too! I can be there in five minutes. I don't want to sully my home's happiness with talk of Slader."

"That is totally understandable."

"See you in a bit, cutie. Is your face red yet?"

"I think everything is under control. See you in a little while." Dupree hung up and said, "Five minutes."

Carr got up and went to the outer office. "I'll wait out here in this lonely old chair. More official."

A minute later there was a pounding on the outer door.

"Why's the door locked? You think he'll come back for another go at you?" Marsh Peterson laughed and came into the office. "Oh, sorry, I didn't know you actually got clients."

"Marsh Peterson, this is detective Carr from the State Police."

Carr stood and faced Marsh. "You're on my list of folks to see. Thanks for saving me the trouble of hunting you down."

"Do I need a lawyer?"

"Why? You have done something I don't know about?"

"Other than beatin' the shit out of the guy trying to kill our friend here? Nothing I can think of."

"Good, no lawyer, needed," Carr said.

"I'll wait in there." Dupree indicated his office.

"Have a seat," Carr said, taking a scarred, leather notebook from his pocket as he sat down.

"Where?"

"I was joking. This will only take a second." Carr looked down at his notebook. "Marsh Peterson, process server with the county court, duly licensed in the state, concealed weapon permit, and no criminal record. That about right?"

"Yes, sir."

"So tell me what happened to Mr. Dupree two days ago."

"I came in to report completed service of papers on Jeremy Epperson, and found him standing over Dupree in there kicking his ribs in."

"What was Mr. Dupree doing?"

"Not much. Mostly trying to protect himself. He was kind of curled up." Marsh leaned in and whispered, "He's not much of a fighter, I don't think."

"What did you do at this point?"

"Yelled for him to stop."

"Epperson."

"Yes."

"Just to be clear. Then?"

"He called me a hobbit. That pissed me off. Then he gave poor Dupree another couple of kicks. I figured he wasn't going to stop." Marsh thought of how to proceed for a long moment.

"Then?"

"Then I gave it to him."

"Jumped in to help Mr. Dupree, you mean."

"Yeah, I knocked Epperson off him. He turned on me and then I dissuaded him enough to get him to stop resisting. That's within my rights. Citizen's arrest kind of deal."

"Did you call the police?"

"What for? All we got around here is the worthless deputy, and they're best friends. Wouldn't have done no good."

"What happened to Jeremy Epperson at this point?"

"He left, lickin' his wounds."

"Anything else to add?" Carr asked, closing his notebook.

"Yeah, why don't you people do something about that deputy and his crooked uncle?"

"Another case. But rest assured, we're on it."

The door opened and Dara stood for a moment looking into the office.

"Sorry, am I interrupting?"

"No, no come in, Mr. Dupree is in his office," Carr said, smiling for the first time. "Thank you, Mr. Peterson, for your cooperation."

Dupree came out into the outer office. "Did you need to see me, Marsh?"

"Nothing special, I just wanted to come see how you were fairin'."

"Thanks to you, much better than I could have been. I actually feel a lot better today."

"All right then. I've done my good deed for the day, and my civic duty. I'll be going." Marsh gave a nod and went to the door. "Want me to lock it?" he asked, laughing as he left the office.

"Funny guy," Carr said, rolling his eyes. "Ms. Walker, nice to see you again. I wish it was over coffee and that amazing banana nut bread of yours."

"I'm sorry I didn't recognize the name or I would have brought you some." Dara smiled.

Carr was like a schoolboy talking to the prettiest girl in class. "No bribing an officer of the law, ma'am." He gave Dara a crooked smile exposing badly stained teeth.

"We mustn't be accused of that," she flirted gently.

"Shall we?" Dupree interrupted.

"I'll grab that chair," Carr offered.

"Sorry about the phone," Dara whispered. "It was just too easy. I could just see you coloring up."

"You are a laugh a minute." Dupree grinned.

"Here we go," Carr said, entering the room chair in hand. "I don't want to put you ill at ease, Ms. Walker."

"Dara, please."

"Thank you, Dara. Like I was saying, this is just a chance for us to talk a bit, for you to make a statement, and me to ask a few questions. Mr. Dupree is here as your legal counsel in case I get out of line."

"I can't imagine," Dara replied.

"All the same, we thought it might be more comfortable for you." Carr shifted his weight in the chair. "For the record, you are..."

"Dara Marie Walker."

"I got your address as 114 Contentment Street, White Owl."

"Correct."

"I am investigating accusations against a Travis Slader, Deputy Sheriff. I want to get a statement from you on an incident that involved Mr. Dupree. For the record, Mr. Dupree has filed a formal complaint and named you as a witness. What can you tell me, about that incident?"

Dara straightened in her chair and took a deep breath. "My husband Mitchell Walker died in an accident fifteen years ago last August. Since that time Mr. Slader has insisted that he will marry me. To be clear, I have not dated, encouraged, or even been particularly nice to Travis Slader. I do not like him, and would never consider any kind of personal relationship with him. I have repeatedly refused his offers to go out with him, and have rejected his delusional belief that 'as soon as I am over my grief' I will marry him. Over the years, he has told members of the community and my customers that I am his fiancé, which I must tell you, is not only embarrassing but infuriating."

"And this started how long after the death of your husband?"

"A week after the funeral. At first, he was kind. He even brought me a card once. At that time I told him I wasn't ready to consider any kind of relationship. He backed off for a couple of months, then it became a constant thing. I have told him no as forceful as I know how. I've actually gotten to the point where I pretend he isn't even there when he starts in.

"The day Dupree got involved, his obsession with me was reaching an almost violent level. It had been building for that last month or so. He insisted we be married. He caused a scene in the café several times in the last year. Calling me darling and sweetheart, and pleading that I marry him on the weekend, or an upcoming holiday. On several occasions, I got angry and even yelled at him."

"I can't blame you. And Mr. Dupree's involvement?"

"Sorry. Travis was ranting about how long he had been saving himself for me, and fifteen years was long enough, and what was I waiting for, and he was just out of control. He scared off most of the customers. I was alone with the cook, TJ my waitress, and a couple in a back booth. That's when Dupree walked in." Dara turned and smiled at Dupree. "To my shock, Mr. Dupree pretended to be my boyfriend. He approached me behind the counter and gave me a peck on the cheek. He asked me what was happening. It seemed to push the deputy over the edge. I got out of the way."

"You did that?" Carr asked in astonishment, looking over at Dupree.

"I sized up an unpleasant situation and that's what I came up with," Dupree explained.

"Please go on, Miss Walker."

"Like I said, I tried to get out of the way. I couldn't figure out who this total stranger was coming to my rescue. I went into the kitchen and got a loaf of nut bread and a big knife."

"What were you going to do with the knife?" Carr asked.

"I'm not sure, protection I guess."

"The deputy was armed."

"Yeah, well it was getting crazy. I told Travis I was refusing him service and telling him to never come into the café again. At that point, Dupree told him that ignoring my request would be trespassing and he would get a restraining order, and have him arrested."

"That ended it?"

"Pretty much," Dara answered, "except when Travis left, he told Dupree he was a dead man."

"Are those his exact words?"

"Yes, sir."

"Well, I guess that's all I need." Carr folded his notebook. "I don't suppose I have to tell you to not make contact with Mr. Slader. Just the same, try and stay out of his way. I know that's hard in a small town like this..."

"What do you intend to do?"

"Words are a funny thing, Dara. I think we have a pretty clear case of harassment, stalking, and the threat of bodily harm. We've got witnesses by the dozen, I imagine? My next move is to get his side of the story. The tricky part is, this was off duty. Has he ever harassed you in uniform?"

"Oh, yes, many times."

"Good." Carr stood. "I never figured one of my last cases would be dealing with sexual harassment by a cop, good god." He sighed. "I'll be in touch."

"Thank you, detective." Dara stood and offered Carr her hand.

As he shook it he said, "You realize I can't arrest him. I can only file a report. A board of review will force the sheriff's hand. If he doesn't act, it will become a state matter. It could take a while."

"All the same, the community needs shed of him. He is a menace." Dara was forceful, yet her compassion for her town came through.

After Carr left, Dara turned to Dupree. "Walk me out?"

"I was hoping you might stick around."

"Things to do. You owe me dinner, remember."

"I won't forget," Dupree replied.

They walked down the stairs in silence. At the street door, Dupree took Dara's wrist. "It's going to be okay."

"I'm not worried. I'll catch you later."

Dupree watched as she walked away. Suddenly she stopped and turned. "I meant what I said about being cute." She flashed him a brilliant smile and went on down the street.

The sky was clear, and Dupree felt the possibilities of a more positive future. He liked Carr and didn't find him nearly as harsh or cantankerous as the secretary warned. He was old school, just the facts ma'am, Joe Friday kind of cop. Dupree knew well how slow the wheels of justice turn, but he hoped Travis Slader would be an exception. He knew it would probably not happen. For Dara's sake, he hoped he was wrong.

"What are you doing back here?"
"I'm a Bust Boy now," Toby answered proudly.
"Your mother knows you got out?"
"I'm supposed to start work today."
"Didn't you see the place is boarded up?"
"Why?"
"Somebody broke all the windows. Was it you?" Slader took out his gun.
"Don't shoot! I'm a good boy!" Toby began to cry.
"I think you broke the windows with a slingshot."
"Not me, not me, not me!"
"Get on back to your bench, you stupid monkey-brained idiot."
Toby didn't hesitate, he ran as fast as he knew how to the end of the building and around the corner.
Slader holstered his weapon and laughed madly.
He walked back around the building to find a man in a navy-blue suit leaning on his cruiser.
"Can I help you?" Slader growled.
Carr held up his badge and State Police ID.
Slader stood a little straighter and said excitedly, "How can I help you?"
"You can answer a few questions. First off, what are you doing here? Second, what did you say to that poor handicapped kid?"

"I saw him prowling around, went to check it out. I must've scared him, he's retarded. Doesn't take much."

"Uh, huh." Carr's tone showed his disbelief in Slader's explanations. "Do you know the owner of this café?"

"I should, she's my fiancé," Slader said proudly.

"Is that right? What do you know?" Carr crossed his arms. "So what can you tell me about this?" Carr flipped his index finger toward the boarded-up walls.

"Somebody shot them out with a Wrist Rocket."

"That's pretty specific. How do you know?"

"What's a few broken windows got to do with the State Police? We handle our own investigations." Slader said indignantly.

"Just answer the question."

"Well, ball bearings were found inside."

"Did you fingerprint them?"

"Well, no."

"What did you do with them?"

"Threw them away."

"And just why would you do that? Throw valuable evidence away, I mean."

"What are you getting at?" Slader was beginning to show signs of his frustration.

"Nothing, should I be?"

"I don't like your tone," Slader snapped.

"OK, let's talk about something else. Do you know Jeremy Epperson?"

"Yeah."

"Well?"

"Well, I guess." Slader's eyes flashed around the parking lot like a trapped animal.

"You guess? I was told you've been best friends all your lives. Is that right?"

"Yeah, so?"

"So, nothing. What are you getting so upset about, Deputy? These are pretty easy questions."

"You sound like you're accusing me of something. It's making me nervous."

"Why? All I asked was if you knew Dara Walker, your best friend, and what happened to the windows? I could ask the same questions to a total stranger sitting at the counter in there."

Slader clenched his teeth, and Carr could see the muscles in his jaw flexing.

"OK, let's cut the crap. Why'd your buddy, Epperson, beat up Dupree the lawyer?"

"He's sticking his nose in a lot of stuff that doesn't concern him."

"Like what? What justifies three broken ribs?"

"He's helping Robin, Jeremy's wife, with a divorce."

"Isn't that what lawyers do? Especially for women who are the objects of physical abuse?"

"She's a liar."

"Why didn't you arrest him?"

"Who?"

"Epperson, you know exactly who." Carr was losing his patience.

"A guy beat him up. I was going to arrest him for assault."

"But not your friend."

"He's the one who got beat up!"

"What about Dupree?"

"He had it coming." Slader realized immediately he said the wrong thing.

"Really? Or was it because he embarrassed you in front of your fiancé? Who, I believe, wants absolutely nothing to do with you and has refused to ever serve you again."

"That's bullshit. It was a misunderstanding. She loves me and I love her." Slader was shifting back and forth on the sides of his boots.

Carr was still leaning in the same position as when the conversation began. "You know what I think?"

"What's that?" Slader asked defiantly.

"I think you broke the windows because Dara wants nothing to do with you, and you were mad. I think you poked and prodded your buddy until he went after Dupree. And, I think you are going to be referred to as the guy who used to be a deputy."

"You can't prove any of that stuff. You don't know who you're messing with. My uncle..."

"Yeah, I heard. I figure he will turn on you in a hot second, rather than lose his cushy setup. The sheriff will probably have forgotten your name by the time this all it gets to his desk. That's what I think."

"It ain't gonna happen. My uncle will stick by me. All this stuff is just he said, she said."

"Except for the witnesses," Carr said dryly.

"It's all because of the lawyer, isn't it?"

"Never tell somebody they're a dead man. Real bad idea in front of witnesses. Look, you've got two options. One, resign, get a job somewhere else, and save a little of your dignity. Two, let me file my report and get a state reprimand requesting your dismissal sent to the sheriff. Either way, you're through bullying, harassing, and generally annoying this town." Carr moved away from the patrol car. "And deputy, don't do anything foolish. Cops don't do well in prison." Carr walked back up the street toward Dupree's office.

Deputy Sheriff Travis Slader was stunned. He stood staring at the back of the man who just shattered his world. His breathing was shallow, his fingertips tingled. It was the lawyer, he thought. I should have run over him. He rubbed his forehead and nearly knocked off his hat.

"I'll call Uncle Phil, he'll set this guy straight." Slader's words sounded hollow in the empty parking lot. "I'll take off. I'll go to California. No, no I can't, my stuff, my apartment." He was beginning to hyperventilate. "Oh, God this is bad. My dad will kill me."

The sound of an approaching car drew Slader's attention. A large white Ford Crown Victoria was coming toward him from the far end of town. He could see, as it got closer, it was a probation department car. Funny, they usually call when they're coming to town, he thought.

The car began to slow and as it rolled by, the probation officer in the front passenger seat called from his open window, "Hey Slader, got a violation. Call you later."

As the car slowly rolled by, Slader saw Jeremy Epperson looking out the back window at him. His friend's eyes told the whole story. He was finished. The guilt in his eyes made it clear Jeremy ratted out his best friend. His lifelong partner in crime, confidant, and companion on a thousand drunken nights, gave him up. Their eyes locked, and for a second Slader thought he saw his friend's lips move. Then Jeremy put his head down and rested it on the cold mesh grill in front of him. Then the car was gone.

"Those bitches! It's all their fault! She's made that lawyer believe he matters. She's used him to get to me. We'll see about that." Slader threw his fist in the air and yelled at the top of his lungs toward the back of the detective still moving up the street, "I'm not done yet!" No one heard him.

Carr touched base with Dupree, giving a quick report on their conversation.

"I rattled him pretty good. I don't think he'll bother anybody for a long while. Probation picked up Epperson, so productive day."

"Thanks for your help," Dupree said.

"I'm going to check in at Grammy's, then go for a drive. See you at supper."

"Fried chicken tonight!" Dupree replied.

When Carr was gone, Dupree went back to the task he began early in the day, writing his resignation letter to Atherton, Miller, and Chase. He started twice and threw away the drafts.

He struggled with the wording, he choked on the explanation, and he felt he wasn't conveying the reasons for his departure. In the time that passed since he dropped the keys on the front seat of his car in the rest stop, life's meaning changed and changed again.

The problem he was learning with each new draft wasn't Diane, though she was a catalyst for action. It wasn't his work, colleagues, or the firm. The problem was him.

The emptiness of a life built on greed, ambition, and the unquenchable need for acceptance and prestige was what drove him away. As he looked down on the yellow legal pad, he wondered how many he filled for other people. Cases where neither side was necessarily right, injured, or wronged. Big companies bullying smaller companies into closure, merger, or bankruptcy. Not the noblest of professions, he thought.

He couldn't write that though, his partners would never understand his conversion to telling the truth, not drinking, and helping people. If he told them he did his first two cases pro bono they would write him off as insane. He couldn't tell them he was living in a room in a boarding house and having dinner every night with a group of oddballs and a bawdy old lady.

He couldn't tell them either that he dipped into the Cloud for legal forms to set up a living trust to save a family farm. 'Where is the profit there?' they would ask. It was the total disregard for profit that Dupree embraced the most in his new life. There would come a time, probably the next client through the door that he would have to bill. The fee would be based on their ability to pay, not a rigid scale. He would take payments, not a retainer. There is enough money in his secret account, and the monies he would receive from the firm, to last him ten lifetimes in White Owl.

How can you tell people, as lost as you were, the error of their ways? After all, he wasn't an evangelist selling salvation, though his decision was his salvation. Could he tell them of the morning he left, how he planned to kill himself? He poked the yellow pad as tears welled up in his eyes.

Could he have done it? Could he have destroyed what is now a contented man? Even with the conflicts he faced since his arrival in White Owl, he made friends. He thought of Terry and the twins, Marsh, Pete Olson downstairs, and Toby. Would he enrich their lives by simply being alive? Then there was Dara.

He was not by nature an amorous man. It wasn't that he was not interested in sex, he was just apathetic from Diane's years of indifference. Diane was exciting for about the first ten times they made love. Then he realized the mechanical, disconnected, passionless activity it was for her.

There was a young intern years ago that he fell hopelessly in love with. She was from a poor family, wore slightly out of date clothes, and worked like a slave. She would pull her hair behind her ear, and to Dupree's younger self it was the most erotic thing he ever saw. He would watch her in the law library reading. He loved the way she would push her glasses up on her nose.

He found himself fantasying about Diane's death in a house fire, plane crash, or boating accident. The intern would come to him in his darkest hour of grief and declare her love, and they would live happily ever after. The scenarios he would play out and bill to some poor unsuspecting client never involved making love. The central desire was her company and her longing to be with him in a life they built together.

She left without even learning her name. He stood watching as she bid farewell to the secretaries and other interns one afternoon. Dupree caught his reflection in the glass he watched her through. She was a kid, probably twenty years younger than him. When their eyes met, she gave him a wave of complete indifference, no feeling, and devoid of any emotional connection. She never noticed he existed. He was so embarrassed he went into his office, closed the door, and wept.

Now he found a beautiful, vibrant woman with a smile that took his breath away. Perhaps she was just being friendly. Perhaps she was a flirt, and he was new and different from the men in town. Perhaps she was just as lonely and needy as he is.

She had her great love. Dupree never had. She might be his first, but he might not measure up, be the wrong shape to fill the hole in her heart longing for a replacement. If she could learn to care for him, he would overcome his self-doubt. He would share this new life with dedication and total commitment. That's silly, he thought. You are doing the whole intern thing again.

He looked down at the scribbling on the yellow pad. Her name was written four times in the margin. What would he tell his partners? A thought struck him. What would he tell his children, should he ever see or talk to them again? The idea frightened him. They were still young. What if they woke up someday and realized what they were, and what their mother made them. It would never happen; he shook his head hard at the thought.

Like in the old movie The Stepford Wives, they were trained and set in their ways. Dupree suddenly came to a painful place he had not visited since he left L.A. He grieved for the character and future of his children. If he could speak to them he would tell them to run. Move to the mountains, become a world traveler, hitchhike, meet real people, get their nose broken if necessary. Break the mold, and free themselves from Satan's chains of their mother's narcissistic world view.

What were these feelings, the pain, and regret, the guilt, and rejection of what was? Were his thoughts the birth pangs of a new life? He was being reborn into a new world of his own making and freeing himself of the safety of the well-planned womb of false security he fashioned so many years ago.

He would live or die, rise or fall, succeed or fail, based on the concern for others and the desire to share his knowledge, skills, and willingness to help. If Dara was part of this new world, he would thank the Creator every day for the blessing of love. If she was not, he would live knowing that he could draw love and human connection from the friends he made and the people he helped, and be thankful for it.

Dupree tore the top page off the yellow pad and tossed it in the wastebasket, and left the office for the day content that he did the best he could. The letter would come when the words did. He wouldn't force it or coerce it. He would write it when the time was right.

Chapter Nine

"Law office."

"Du'? It's Marty."

Dupree was surprised to hear the voice of his old friend and partner. He looked at the top of his desk for a long moment before saying, "Well, hello."

"What have you done?" Martin Hutchinson spoke with an accusation that hung heavy in the air.

"What do you mean?"

"You know exactly what I mean. Walking off like some character out of an arthouse movie."

"I decided I didn't want to kill myself after all. So, I simply left the cause of my hopelessness behind. Simple as that."

"Kill yourself?" Martin Hutchinson was stunned. "What do you mean? I thought you were the most together person I know."

"That is the point old friend, I wasn't. I hated my home and was dragging the firm around like a yoke and plow. I couldn't go on the way things were. I got up one morning and decided to end it all. I was going to leave the car running in the garage. Then I realized Diane would probably open the door and ruin it like she has ruined my life. So when I was supposed to turn right to go to the office, I turned left."

"Just like that."

"Just like that," Dupree confirmed.

"What about the car, I mean, how did you get to, whatever it is, Washington?"

"Hitchhiked."

"You? Hitchhiked? The guy who always insists on driving?"

"All the way to Williams, California, then I took the train. And a bus," Dupree said as an afterthought.

"I'm sorry, but, I, I'm just a bit taken aback by all this. At first, I thought you were carjacked, or something worse. Then I thought, maybe you just needed a break, some space, you know? But this, I just..."

"I did need space. From everyone and everything in my life. I saw it as them or me. So I chose me. Marty, I'm not coming back."

"So where does that leave the firm?"

"I spent most of the day yesterday composing a letter trying to explain myself. I threw every draft away. The simple truth, it seems, is I don't care."

"That's great, I worry myself sick and it turns out you don't give a shit. Terrific."

"You're missing the greater point. You could be having this conversation with Diane over my grave. Would you prefer that?" Dupree showed his displeasure for the first time.

"Of course not. So, what am I supposed to do?"

Dupree didn't even hesitate. "Anything liquid that's mine, give it to Diane. Freeze the retirement account at its present value. Take my name off the door and letterhead. Give my current cases to Gutierrez, he's a good kid and will make a great partner someday."

"That's it?"

"Can you think of anything else?"

"Do you want me to represent you in the divorce?"

"No, I already signed the papers. I gave her everything. There is enough in our checking and saving to last her a long time. If not, that's her problem."

"Just like that?"

"Just like that."

"What are you going to do?"

"Doing it. I've opened a small practice, here in White Owl. I've met some nice folks too. It's going to be alright."

"And you're sure you're OK?"

"You mean, have I had some kind of a mental breakdown?" Dupree laughed. "I have never felt better or been more lucid in my life. You should try it."

"Right. How will I send you the paperwork for all this?"

"Unless you're going to fight it, here is my fax number." Dupree gave Hutchinson the number, then continued, "I really meant no harm, you need to understand that."

"It's just a lot to wrap my head around. I must say, you stuck with Diane a hell of a lot longer than I could have." Hutchinson finally relaxed a bit. "I'll present this to the partners. I don't expect a problem."

"Why don't you and Chrissie come up and see me. It is truly God's country up here. You'd be surprised what it does for your outlook."

"We just might do that. I'll talk to you later." Hutchinson paused. "I really do wish you well."

"That means a lot. See ya." Dupree set the handset on its base.

Dupree just shut the last door. His course was set and there would be no going back. He leaned back in his chair and laced his fingers behind his head.

"This place needs a radio," he said, staring at the ceiling.

A few minutes later Dupree was out on the sidewalk looking up and down the street.

"You lost?" Pete Olson asked from the door of his store.

"Good morning Pete, where would I go to buy a radio, or boom box or something? The silence up there is driving me buggy."

"The furniture store I suppose. We don't get a lot of stations here. You'd be better off with Pandora on your computer."

"How's that work?"

"Wait until Jennifer gets here and I'll come up and set it up for you."

"That would be wonderful." Dupree smiled.

From a distance, the sound of an approaching siren cut through the quiet of the morning.

"What do you suppose that's about?" Olson asked.

"Police. Fire?"

"Fire. They don't get a lot of calls. Emergency medical stuff mostly."

As the sound grew louder, the two men watched up the street. The red volunteer fire department truck sped by the intersection and a moment later the siren stopped.

"Be right back," Dupree said, as he walked quickly toward the last sound of the siren.

Toby Wharton came running around the corner and nearly ran into Dupree. He was obviously agitated and Dupree could see he was crying.

"Toby, Toby are you okay?"

"I can't be a Bust Boy today! I can't be a Bust Boy today again!" he panted, running past Dupree.

The sight as he rounded the corner stopped Dupree. Up the street, the end of the Firetruck was protruding from the back of The Quarter Moon. Smoke billowed into the clear blue sky. Dupree broke into a run.

A second siren was approaching, Dupree was unsure from what direction. There was something painted across the plywood on the front of the building but from his vantage point, Dupree couldn't read it. A few more yards and the message read clearly and hatefully. LYING BITCHES was scrawled across the front of the café in bold, black spray paint.

The Sheriff's department cruiser flew past Dupree and screeched to a stop at the corner of The Quarter Moon. Slader got out of the car and looked back at Dupree. Without a word or any recognition, he moved around the corner and out of sight.

For a moment, Dupree wasn't sure how to proceed. A small white car pulled up to the curb, and Burt Carr rolled down his window.

"It just doesn't let up," Carr grumbled. "How stupid is this guy? Look at that!" Carr pointed at the front of the building. "Is there anyone else in this state that would do that?"

"He's the only one I can think of." Dupree shook his head in disgust.

"You probably shouldn't go over there. I'll take a look and let you know. Why don't you call Dara?"

"Alright, that's probably best."

"Of course, he might take a swing at you if you were to pop off something smart, then I could arrest him!" Carr chuckled and pulled away from the curb.

Dupree stood watching Carr pull in beside Slader. Before Dupree could decide what to do, Slader came around the corner of the building and got in his car. The engine roared and the car was slammed in reverse, throwing gravel everywhere as he spun around and headed back towards Dupree.

A dozen scenarios flew through Dupree's mind, from Slader shooting Carr and coming after him, to Slader leaving town. None of his ideas came close to what he was actually about to witness. The cruiser screamed around the corner sliding and fishtailing. The breaks were applied so hard that the car slid, and Slader bolted from the car in front of Wharton's Furniture.

Without fully processing what he was doing, Dupree broke into a run. All he could think of was Slader somehow abusing Toby. As he reached the front doors he grabbed the metal frame of the door and swung into the furniture store. He could hear yelling in the direction of the office. A moment later, Slader appeared, shoving Toby forward.

The boy was handcuffed and Karen Wharton was behind Slader, crying and screaming.

"What are you doing?" Dupree demanded as the three people reached where he stood. Placed firmly in the aisle, Slader was given no choice but to stop or knock him down.

"Out of the way!" Slader yelled.

"Not until you give me an explanation for this!" Dupree stood his ground.

"None of your business. But if you must know, this retard set fire to the café." Slader glared at Dupree.

"Don't be ridiculous."

"Do something, Mr. Dupree." Karen pleaded.

"Don't worry. We'll get this straightened out."

"Yeah, at the trial," Slader remarked.

"His or yours?"

"Out of the way."

"Mom!" Toby cried. He was in a complete state of panic.

"Don't talk to him, Toby. Keep silent." Dupree tried to be reassuring. "Do you understand?"

"Mom!" Toby screamed so hard it sounded as if he was tearing his vocal cord.

Slader shoved Toby hard and he slammed into Dupree as they went past.

"Get your car, Karen. We'll follow them."

"This way!" Karen turned and ran for the back doors. Dupree followed and in moments they were out the back door and getting in the Wharton's car. Jack Wharton stood motionless in the office door, with no sign of emotion or concern.

The deputy's car went by the end of the alley as Karen raced to catch up. In the split-second Dupree had to respond, he reached over and blared the horn at Burt Carr as he was getting into his car. In that fleeting moment, Carr saw Dupree wave for him to follow.

"Where was Toby before Slader showed up?" Dupree asked softly.

"On his bench, I suppose." Tears streamed down Karen's cheeks.

"Did he say anything about going to work at the café?"

"He talks of nothing else. I've explained he has to wait a few days. He has a real hard time understanding what time is. A day is a week to him sometimes." Karen spoke in bursts between gasping for air.

"Karen, you need to relax. This will all be explained. You need to breathe slowly. No more questions for now. Just relax. Can you do that for me?"

"I'll try."

It took a little over thirty minutes to reach the Stevens County Jail. Slader went through the security fence on the side of the building. Dupree and Karen parked in front.

"Please let me do the talking. I know how upset you are, but cool and calm will win the day." Dupree reached over and patted Karen on the arm. "We can do this."

"Just get him away from that terrible man," she said desperately.

"That's why we're here."

The front desk of the Sheriff's Office was behind thick bulletproof glass. A woman in a department uniform looked up and smiled as Dupree approached the window.

"I need to speak to a booking officer or the highest-ranking department member in the building."

"And you are?" The deputy keyed the microphone in front of her.

"I'm sorry, my name is Dupree, I'm legal counsel for Toby Wharton, who's just being brought in. He is mentally challenged. He has Down syndrome. He is very upset and doesn't understand what is going on. I fear for his safety and health." Dupree was pleasant but very firm.

"Why was he brought in?"

"Deputy Slader claims he set a fire."

"Just a minute." The woman turned off her microphone and punched numbers into a phone. Dupree tried to read her lips but it was futile.

It was several minutes before the deputy returned to Dupree. "Lieutenant O'Connor will be out to talk to you in a moment."

"Thank you." Dupree glanced around the room and directed Karen to a bench against the far wall.

The Lieutenant smiled as he came through the door into the waiting area. He was of average height and weight. Nothing remarkable about him, except for his flaming red hair that was buzzed short, and his short-cropped matching mustache.

"Morning, folks," O'Connor said, approaching the bench where Dupree and Karen now stood.

"Good morning, this is Karen Wharton from White Owl. I am her attorney; my name is Dupree. We are very concerned about her son, Toby, who has been brought in by Deputy Slader. Toby is a young man with special needs, severe mental disabilities, and we are concerned for his emotional, physical, and mental condition as I'm sure can imagine."

"I spoke with Deputy Slader and he is charging Mr. Wharton with arson." O'Connor began. "After booking, he will be released in the care of his caregiver. As I'm sure you can appreciate, arson is a serious crime."

"What evidence does the Deputy have for this arrest?" Dupree asked.

"Mr. Wharton was on the premises yesterday and was asked to leave by Deputy Slader. Today, after the fire was reported, Mr. Wharton was seen running from the premises."

"That's it?" Dupree was trying to control his anger. "Did he have matches? A lighter? An igniter of any kind? Accelerant? Does he smell of smoke or gasoline?" Dupree pressed.

"It will all be in the Deputy's report."

"You people are leaving yourselves wide open for a false arrest, harassment, and discrimination of a handicapped person, and undue trauma of a mentally disabled person suit. I want my client released immediately. I also insist that Deputy Slader be investigated for calling my client a retard."

"He'll be released when he's released and you all can go back to White Owl and you can be a big fish in your little pond again. That big shot act doesn't fly around here. Just who do you think you are? Coming in my offices acting like some hotshot L.A. lawyer off TV!"

"I am a big shot lawyer from L.A.! Google me. You, sir, have just stepped in it. You are going to replay this moment over and over wishing you had called in sick." Dupree took a step closer to the deputy. "You have five minutes to get my client out here." He turned and went back to the bench, sat down, and crossed his legs.

The Lieutenant didn't respond. He shot a fiery glance at the woman behind the glass and she buzzed him in the security door.

"I think you made him angry," Karen whispered.

"Good. He knows we're serious."

Three minutes later Toby came through the security door with a female deputy and a handful of papers.

"I'll take those for you."

"Mom!" Toby called out, seeing Karen.

They embraced and Dupree turned to the Deputy.

"What's your name, Deputy?"

"Why?" she asked suspiciously.

"Because you, my dear, will be named in the lawsuit. I will be filing against your department, the county, and your sheriff."

"Platt. But I..."

"See you in court, Deputy Platt."

Dupree smiled at Karen Wharton and moved toward the door. Toby was weeping softly.

Karen asked Dupree if he would like to drive back to White Owl, and he readily agreed.

"I could use a Frosty," Dupree said, pulling into a Wendy's drive-thru. "How about you two?"

"Yes!" Toby shouted.

"Shhhh. In the car voice, sweetie," Karen said softly. "I think an ice cream would be just the thing right now. Thank you."

The return to White Owl was peaceful and quiet. After finishing his ice cream, Toby fell asleep and slumped against the door. Karen gazed out the window and Dupree wished he could hear her thoughts.

After a few miles, Dupree switched on the radio and found a station with a familiar tune and let it play. As the car approached the White Owl ten-mile sign, it dawned on Dupree that Burt Carr didn't follow them to the jail.

The thirty minutes back to White Owl seemed more like ten as Dupree plotted out his strategy to sue Slader and the Sheriff's Department. The suit was not of particular merit. Toby was not harmed and would probably not suffer any lasting emotional damage. It was, in Dupree's eyes, one more nail in the coffin of Slader's career.

When they arrived back in town, Dupree assured Karen he would be following up on all the papers and file preliminary court documents. He would also contact as many Down Syndrome Organizations he could find in the state, as well as national support groups.

"If you don't mind, I'm going to get out here," Dupree said, as he pulled into the Quarter Moon parking lot. "I think I'll snoop around a bit."

"Please let me know as soon as you know anything, about anything," Karen said, as they crossed paths and she took the driver's seat.

"I promise."

Dupree waited until Karen and Toby pulled away before he turned to face the café. He needed to take a fresh first look at the damage and evidence left behind. From the look of the spray paint lettering, the perpetrator was in no hurry. There was little running of the paint and the letters were uniform. He hopefully looked around for an empty spray can. There was none to be seen. Satisfied with his observations, he walked to the rear of the building.

"Adam! Where have you been? I've been frantic." Dara was examining the damage near the back door.

"Slader arrested Toby Wharton and I went to the jail with his mother. I came to take a look around. What have you found? Anything?"

"That poor kid didn't do this," she said confidently. "This was set by someone who planned it, and knew exactly what they were doing." She squatted down, "Look at this."

Leading to the back door was a black trail of six to eight feet of burned accelerant and a pile of ashes. The ashes were the remains of newspapers and shopping bags.

"I don't have trash back here. There's the dumpster." Dara pointed to a fenced area at the end of the lot. "This stuff was brought with the purpose of setting a fire. Toby, God bless him, simply isn't smart enough to plan this out. He was here to go to work."

"Slader did this, I'd bet anything I own. That's his work out front too." Dara stood, whirled around and kicked the dirt.

"I will be filing a suit, claiming false arrest, discrimination of the handicapped, harassment, and anything else I can think of along the way. That sheriff's department will want to burn him at the stake when I'm through."

"And in the meantime, what happens to me?" Dara snapped.

"In the meantime, you go on with life, get the café reopened, and let me worry about the deputy. I will file for a restraining order. Even Slader isn't stupid enough to ignore that. He's going to have so many cans tied to his tail he will have no choice but to get as far from here as he can."

Dara was not convinced. "I have known him for a long time. He is twisted and has some serious issues when it comes to the people of this town. He is getting worse by the day. I'm afraid for you, and I am afraid for me. I don't want anything to happen to you, Adam."

"And I don't want anything to happen to you, either. I will do everything I can to get rid of this guy once and for all."

Without warning, Dara threw her arms around Dupree's neck and held him tightly. "I think I'm falling in love with you," she whispered. "Don't say anything, please. Just let me speak. I have lost one man I loved, I would die if I lost another."

Dupree wrapped his arms around Dara's waist and pulled her close to him. Her words carried a meaning that eluded him his whole life. Diane occasionally muttered a quick 'I love you' when she got a present or her way about something, but it could easily have been 'thanks a lot.' Dara spoke the feeling of her heart, a well thought out statement that meant he was important to her, that he filled a void, long empty and aching to be filled.

He turned his head ever so slightly and kissed her softly on the neck. She pulled back and kissed him full on the lips, deep, long, and hard. When she pulled back, she released his arms. Dupree held her for a moment longer, then released his grasp as well. She reached out and took him by both hands and looked up into his eyes.

"If we can't rid ourselves of this man, I would go anywhere you choose. I think we could be happy anywhere. I have some savings, and I can sell the café. People ask all the time. Please don't be all alpha male and not tell me if you can't do it. I don't care. We are happiness. Do you understand?"

Dupree nodded and smiled. "I promise, if I see that he will win, I will find us somewhere wonderful. I promise."

Dara let go of his hands. "You said you have work to do?"

"Yeah, I have."

"The glass should be here shortly." Dara cut him off. "I'll stay here. Can I come to see you when they finish?"

"You better." Dupree smiled.

The sound of a car crunching gravel made Dupree turn around. It was Carr.

"You didn't follow us."

"Who?"

"Karen Wharton and I waved at you."

"I must not have had my driving glasses on. I can't see distances without them. When was this?"

"Never mind, it turned out to not matter."

"I hear that your buddy arrested that poor kid that sits on the bench all day."

"Toby. Yeah, hauled him to the jail in Colville. The whole place is rotten. The lieutenant between the uncle and the sheriff could have cared less his deputy cuffed a kid with Down syndrome and booked him for arson."

"There is no way in hell that simpleminded kid set that fire. This is not a case of some kid playing with matches. This was premeditated, and they used a pretty sophisticated ignition device." Carr reached in his pocket and pulled out a plastic evidence bag. "Swear to god, you'd think that deputy was the retarded one. Excuse me. Old habits die hard, mentally challenged one." Carr winced. "This is a remote spark used for keeping your distance from heavily fuel-doused brush fires. Works up to a half-mile."

"So, Slader could be talking to somebody, flick the switch, and have an alibi that places him far from the fire."

"You got it."

"That's why Toby was so scared. He went around to knock on the back door, and the wall goes up in flames around him."

"It would scare the shit out of me," Carr agreed. "The arson could have set the kid on fire, adding murder to the charges."

"Poor Toby," Dara said. "What a morning for him."

"So how will you proceed?" Dupree asked.

"I have a call in for a search warrant of Slader's cruiser and residence. Being the weekend, I don't expect to hear back until Monday. He's not what you call a flight risk. Probably figures he's pulled off a good one."

"Not in my book," Dara said angrily.

"I would think not. Look, I got some sniffing around to do. I'll see you later."

"Thanks, Burt," Dara said, as he turned.

"Anything for a pretty lady!" Carr was walking away but waved his hand high in the air.

"See, we've got a good man on the case."

"Two," Dara smiled.

The thrill of real law came flooding back as Dupree reviewed the paperwork from the jail. He found several errors and a few typos, but the main points were clear. Toby was told by Slader the day before to stay away from the café until it reopened. He saw Toby running from the building in a state of agitation.

"That's impossible," Dupree said aloud. "He drove by after Toby ran past me on the sidewalk! I gotcha!"

It was after three when Dara came to join Dupree at the office. She brought a tape measure and busied herself in the front office, formulating her ideas for a more welcoming and less empty space.

A short while later they were joined by Burt Carr. He looked tired and his color was bad.

"Are you alright, Burt?" Dara asked as he came into the office.

"Time to retire, I guess."

"I'll get you something to drink." Dara grabbed her purse and was out the door.

Carr went into Dupree's office and collapsed into a chair. His pallor disturbed Dupree.

"I'm concerned about you, Carr. Maybe we should call a doctor."

"I'll be fine, I just walked farther than I should have, and then those stairs did me in. I'll be right as rain when I get a drink of water. What you got, anything?"

"Slader's arrest statement claims he saw Toby running from The Quarter Moon. That is impossible because Toby ran past me before Slader got to the scene. He lied."

"Of course he did." Carr gave a weak grin.

"With that bit of good news, I think I have enough to file my report. I think after I rest up a bit, I'll head for home."

"Why don't you lie down for a bit? I really am worried about you."

The outer office door closed harder than Dara intended and she joined the men in the office. "Here you go, Burt," she said, handing Carr a bottle of water.

"Thanks." Carr twisted the cap and took a sip of water. Trying to make his movement unnoticeable, he reached in his jacket pocket and took out an orange pill bottle.

"Whatcha got there?" Dara inquired.

"I forgot my meds this morning," Carr said, trying to remove the lid.

"Here, let me help." Dara took the bottle and opened the lid. "Childproof, and adult proof, too." She tried to lighten the mood, as she quickly read the label. "Nitrostat. Something you want to tell us, Burt?"

"I get angina when I overdo or get too stressed. You got me," Carr shrugged. "Maybe I will lay down for a bit. Just until the Nitro kicks in."

"Yeah, go for it. I lay on that old couch all the time," Dupree encouraged.

"You do?" Dara asked in mock surprise. "I thought you were up here working!"

Carr moved to the couch and laid down with a sigh. Dara rested her hands on the chair in front of the desk and gave Dupree a concerned look.

"Come see what I have been doing." Dara jerked her head hard toward the front office.

Without saying anything, Dupree got up and followed Dara.

"He looks awful," Dara whispered.

"Let him rest. If he doesn't snap out of it, I'll insist he gets checked out."

Dara smiled and nodded in agreement. "I thought you could paint this wall a dove gray and this one a contrasting burgundy. It would update the space and make it not quite so gloomy."

"Sounds good." Dupree turned his head toward his office. "He's snoring."

"Let's go for a walk. Let him rest," Dara said softly.

The long shadows of the afternoon sun walked ahead of the couple as they strolled up the street. The conversation was centered on the day's activities. They rounded the corner and as they crossed the street, a Sheriff's Department cruiser passed them. Oddly, it wasn't Slader. An older man was at the wheel and made no sign of recognition when Dara waved a greeting.

"Think that's the uncle?" Dupree asked.

"I don't know. I don't think I've ever seen him. He's from Colville."

As they walked toward The Quarter Moon, Dara reached over and took Dupree's hand.

"I want you to know that none of this is your fault. Really, this mess with Slader has been brewing for a long time. It just happened to boil over when you came into the café. I really don't know what would have happened."

"Are you really that afraid of him?" Dupree asked. "I mean physically afraid? Has he ever tried to touch you?"

"No, but I think he's got a screw loose. When it comes to me, he can't tell his fantasy from reality. So, yeah, he frightens me. I really don't know what he is capable of. It's scary when you can't call the police."

"That's where our friend Carr comes in. He's the big dog, he'll clear all this up," Dupree said, trying to reassure her.

"You really think so?" Dara's voice showed her skepticism.

"Yeah. This is his last case. He wants to go out on a high note. This could be a career-capping legend."

"You talk like it's a game." Dara released Dupree's hand and stopped walking. "He has to end this. Otherwise, this town will dry up and blow away. People are already leaving, and talking about leaving, and it is because of Travis Slader."

"I'm sorry, I wasn't being flippant. I have some tricks up my sleeve as well. There are civil litigations that would cost the county so much to try they would empty the coffers. That would take longer, but in the end, White Owl wins. Deputy Slader would be too much of a liability for the sheriff to protect any longer. Carr's way is faster. Let's let him do his job." Dupree hoped his closing argument would be enough to change the subject. "Now, let's talk about dinner tonight."

"Can't. I have a baby shower to go to with TJ. But, tomorrow night I am preparing dinner for a handsome lawyer at my place. Want to come?"

"I was hoping to get the beautiful owner of the best café in town out of the kitchen for once."

"But she has a really comfy couch that's really nice for snuggling up on." Dara took Dupree's hand again.

"Looks like the prosecution has been outmaneuvered."

"Get used to it, counselor."

Chapter Ten

Travis Slader parked his Camaro almost two blocks from Dara's house, across from Kenny Perry's house at the stop sign. He never paid attention to anything that didn't directly involve him. So, he didn't know the kid he tormented through school was sitting in his front room watching him get out of his car. In a more spiritual world, he would have sensed the hatred that burned in Kenny for him. Slader's focus was on his plan and he would not be distracted, even when the porch light came on above Kenny's door.

The closer Slader got to Dara's house, the faster he walked. The excitement of seeing her and showing her the ring he bought was almost more than Slader could keep inside. He began to hum an old song. The words were eluding him, but the tune seemed like the perfect soundtrack for this moment.

He knew this was the perfect night. The red velvet case rubbed in his pocket. He was excited but calm. The three shots of Jack Daniels helped that. He practiced his speech over and over all day. The answers he prepared for her rejection were pure genius in his mind. Nothing could go wrong. She was going to love his new shirt. Tonight, she'll see how wrong about him she has been.

As he approached Dara's house practicing his speech aloud, the porch light was shining a welcome.

"Good evening, my sweet," he would say. "I have come to speak to you about something very important. May I come in?" He nodded his head in approval of his words. "Now, make sure to speak slow. I know, I know. I got this."

Going to the sidewalk up to the porch would take too long. Slader cut across the yard. At the bottom of the steps he took a deep breath, then quickly ran up the steps to the door. Inside was bright, and it seemed all the lights in the house must be on. He peered through the glass in the front door and could see that the dining room table was set.

Moving to the window left of the door, the setting became more visible. It was set for two.

"That could work," Slader said, as he squared himself with the door and knocked.

His heart was pounding; his calm was turning to a twitchy excitement. There was no answer to his knock. He tried again. Nothing.

From the window on the right side of the door, he thought he might see movement in the kitchen. He left the porch and rounded the left side of the house. He was careful to not make any noise. The kitchen was well lit. He grasped the window sill and pulled himself up the twelve inches to take a quick peek. The kitchen was empty. He could hear water in the pipes. Somewhere in the house water was running.

He continued down the wall. In the back corner, he could see a window higher off the ground and much smaller than the kitchen window. The light through the glass showed it was the frosted glass of a bathroom. Standing below the window, Slader could see steam coming from a three-inch opening. He was too short to jump and grab this sill. He frantically started looking for something he could stand on.

Slader's heart was pounding, and he was breathing heavily when he found a stepladder leaning on the back of the house. He raced back to the window and opened the small wooden ladder.

Dara's voice was coming from the window. She was singing. He couldn't identify the song, but her voice was that of an angel. He climbed the ladder to where he could see through the gap in the open window. Inside he could see Dara's naked body through the steamy frosted glass of the shower. He could see the curves of her body and the outline of her hips. She was washing her hair. Her arms were raised and rinsing her hair under the showerhead. As she turned to rinse the back, her breasts were visible but lacking detail because of the frosted glass. Slader cursed in a harsh whisper.

The love he held so long and so close was turning to a raging lust. He must have her. She was his; the ring in his pocket showed his sincerity. How could he get to her? He must hold her wet naked body. She turned off the shower. He must move, he must take her now. Jumping from the ladder, he ran to the back of the house. The flimsy door on the screened-in back porch was unlocked. He moved quietly into the screened area and up to the back door. He tried the knob. It was locked. He reached in his pocket for his

Buck knife. The old door lock popped open without Slader hardly applying any force. He was in.

The old washroom was dark. Slader moved through the house without making a sound. At the end of the hall, the light of the bathroom was a prism beckoning him onward through the darkness. He held the knife, still in his hand, tightly. The door stood open and Dara's naked form was in front of him. Her back was to him as she dried herself with a large white towel.

"Good evening, my sweet," Slader said as brightly as his breathlessness would allow. "I have come to speak to you about something very important. May I come in?"

Dara whirled about and screamed a terrified cry for help.

"Now, now darling. I'm sorry I startled you. We need to talk."

"Get out of my house!" Dara's eyes flashed pure hate as she glanced around the room for a weapon. As she fixed the towel around her, she spotted what she was looking for. On the sink were the scissors she used to trim her hair before her shower.

In the same instant, Slader saw her eyes land on the weapon. He stepped forward and grabbed her wrist with his left hand the moment she grasped the scissors. She twisted and hit him with her free hand. Wrenching her arm hard, Slader landed a thunderous blow to the left side of her face.

"Be still. You are going to enjoy loving me. Stop it!" Slader demanded.

Dara fought and kicked hard at Slader. He yanked her arm hard toward the ceiling, and slammed her in the stomach with his free hand, knocking the wind out of her. Gasping and struggling for breath, she thrust her knee up, aiming for his groin, but missed the mark, her knee landed mid-thigh.

"I don't want to hurt you. But you're mine and I am having what I've been waiting fifteen years for. You can make love to me or I will beat you 'til you do. I'm sick of you calling the shots!"

Dara spat in Slader's face. He let go of her wrist and hit her hard in the face with his left hand. Her knees buckled and she was losing consciousness.

"Adam," she called as she blacked out, dropping the scissors.

Travis Slader now saw the object of his twisted desire as the towel dropped to the floor. He caught Dara in his arms as she began to collapse to the floor. Sweeping her up in his arms, he went into the hall looking for the bedroom.

Down the street, and unseen, Kenny slipped into the street and followed Slader. There was no reason for Slader to be on his street. As Slader crossed Dara's lawn, Kenny understood his purpose. He knew that Slader was no longer welcome at the café. He knew that Dupree was seeing Dara, and he knew that this would not be an expected visit. Kenny stood in the shadows when Slader pounded on the front door and looked into the front windows.

When Slader slipped around the side of the house, Kenny followed. He watched as Slader put the stepladder up to the bathroom window. Kenny silently cursed him and called him filthy names. He knew he couldn't confront the deputy. Slader proved many times over the years that Kenny's attempts at confrontation would be met with him receiving black eyes and bloody noses. This time there was no Terry to protect him. There were no police to call. No one except himself knew what was happening. Kenny stood in the dark, praying that Slader was not about to do what he feared when he saw him return to the back of the house. When he heard Dara's screams, Kenny ran home in the dark, cursing his cowardice.

Dara's limp body lay on the bed. Slader quickly undressed. He neatly hung his new shirt on the chair against the wall. As he moved to the side of the bed, Dara began to move. Her right eye was swollen shut and the other was swelling. Blood ran from her nose and the corners of her mouth.

"Help!" Dara screamed, and Slader punched her in the face.

"Do that again, you'll get the same."

Dara struggled to get up and Slader punched her in the side. "I told you we are going to be together. You're a strong-willed woman, I get it, but you can't fight the inevitable. Just lay back and enjoy what your man's got for you."

Slader threw his leg across Dara. She spit at him. He wiped his mouth of the bloody spittle and slammed his fist into her face, again and again. He hit her until she was still.

When he finished his disgusting act, Slader walked naked to the bathroom, splashed his face and rinsed his mouth. He picked up Dara's towel from the floor and sniffed it. He smiled and dried his face. When he returned to the bedroom, Dara was still motionless.

"You look like shit," Slader taunted his victim. "If I didn't know who you were, I'd never recognize you." As he dressed, Slader laughed at his joke. "Now, when you heal up and I can stand to look at you, we'll have that little talk." Slader slipped on his boots and left the room.

The path to the front door went past the kitchen, and Slader spotted a tray of vegetables. He crossed the kitchen and took two carrot slices from the tray and dipped them in the bowl of Ranch dressing at the center of the tray.

Slader exited the house through the front door and left it wide open. Then he walked back to his car, right up the middle of the street. He swaggered like a man who had just won the lottery. He hummed the same song as before, but this time the words came back to him, Well, I'm hot-blooded, check it and see, I got a fever of a hundred and three. He sang the words repeatedly, changing the melody and the emphasis on different words, as he chanted.

Kenny Perry sat on his porch in the dark. His wife and kids were at her sister's in Seattle, and he was alone. He cried in burning anger returning to his house. He felt as if Satan was roaming the neighborhood and God was sleeping. This vile creature came onto his street, raped his friend, a woman whose essence was love for the community. She never said an unkind word or turned down a request for help from a stranger. Truth be told, Kenny loved her deeply. He loved who she was, not in a carnal way, but for the beauty in her smile and in her heart.

Hot blooded check it and see… The words floated down the empty street.

At that moment, Kenny knew what he must do. God may be asleep, but he was wide awake, and for the first time in his life he didn't need backup. Kenny Perry was God's avenging angel. This foul stench on his town must be dealt with once and for all. Kenny stood and moved across the lawn to where his truck was parked on a slab next to the fence.

From under the seat of his truck, Kenny took a crowbar he kept there for prying up septic tank lids. He crossed the dark street and stood behind the old cottonwood in the front yard of an empty rental. The crowbar's iron felt good in his hand, like a baseball bat that knew a home run was about to win the game.

Got a fever of a hundred and three, three, three. Travis Slader fumbled for his keys in the front pocket of his jeans.

"Remember me?" Kenny asked as he stepped up behind Slader. "Your turn to piss your pants."

Slader turned with a condescending sneer on his face. The force of the crowbar slamming across his mouth broke his jaws and crushed his teeth. Slader's head snapped back. The second blow hit Slader on the top of the head like a log being split for firewood. The power of the blow sent splinters of bone and cold steel into his brain. He fell dead to the pavement.

Kenny walked calmly to his truck, started the engine and backed up to where Slader lay. Moving quickly and with purpose, Kenny opened the side cargo door of his tanker truck. With strength only a rush of adrenalin can bring, he grabbed Slader under the arms and shoved him into the empty storage space. Returning to the cab, Kenny grabbed his flashlight. Quickly but efficiently he shined the light, looking for anything that might say Slader was there. The light caught several fragments of bones, teeth, and brains, and lots of blood. Without hesitation, Kenny took the broom from the side of his truck and the hard-plastic dustpan and swept up any and all signs of the slaughter. Using the high-pressure sanitation hose on the truck, he sprayed a biodegradable bacteria-killing solution over the area. No smell, no DNA problems, Kenny thought.

The flashlight again swept the pavement. Nothing. Kenny climbed into the cab and drove down the street, lights off and engine softly accelerating.

At five minutes to seven, Dupree came through the back fence of Grammy's headed for Dara's. There was a different feeling tonight. The nervous first date jitters were gone. They kissed, rather she kissed him. There was no doubt she was interested in his affection. She moved first. That was a new kind of feeling for Dupree, and he liked it.

The street seemed darker than usual. Dara's porch light was like a lighthouse in the darkness. The houses on both sides of the street were dark. The silence was unnerving. No dogs, no cars passing, just the still of a Sunday night. Dupree didn't notice the door was open until he was on the porch.

"Dara!" He called through the open door.

There was no response. Dupree entered the house and closed the door behind him. He saw the table was set. He moved to the kitchen. There was food on the counter waiting to be cooked and heated. He saw the veggie tray. He glanced around the room. She's in the bathroom, he thought. It was then he saw a stream and then a dribble of ranch dressing across the floor. Dupree smiled.

He returned to the dining room area and listened. The house was quiet. He waited for several minutes. There was no sound, no toilet flushing, no closets closing.

"Dara. Where are you?"

It was then he heard a faint sound. At first, he wasn't sure he heard anything. Maybe it was just a house noise. He moved toward the dark hall. He heard the sound again. This time he was sure.

"Adam." It was a faint, almost muffled sound.

He moved quickly down the hall. The bathroom light flooded the hallway. Dupree moved to the light. The shower door was open and a towel lay on the floor. A sick feeling came over Dupree. Something was desperately wrong.

He returned to the hall.

"Adam." The voice was Dara, and it was coming from just down the hall. Moving to the open door, he stood peering into the darkness.

"Dara?"

"Help me, please." Dara wanted to get up, tried to get up, but all she could manage was to grab a corner of the sheet to cover herself. Her only thought was not letting Dupree see her in such a state.

Dupree fumbled for a light switch. He couldn't find one and blindly entered the room. His leg bumped the bed and Dara groaned. Blindly he reached out and felt a lamp next to the bed. Finding the switch, he flicked the light on.

From a mass of rumpled bedding, the face of a stranger turned from the light. Dara's face was swollen nearly round, and a swirl of deep purple bruises and dark open wounds. Both of her eyes were swollen shut. Her lips were split and huge with swelling.

"Adam, is that you?"

"Yes, darling. It's me. What happened! Who did this to you?"

"I love you, Adam. Please don't let me die," she panted.

"You're not going to die. I'm here. We will get you help. I'm here, and I love you too." Dupree's voice cracked and he began to weep silently. He slipped his arm under Dara's back and held her to him. She began to cry.

"Hold me."

"I have you. I'll never let you go." With his free hand, Dupree strained to reach the phone on the nightstand. He used his thumb to punch 911.

"I need an ambulance," he said as calmly as he could. He gave the address. "And, please call Detective Burt Carr at the State police. Give him this number."

"Please stay on the line, sir."

Dupree dropped the phone on the bed and wrapped both arms around Dara.

Moments later the sound of a siren cut through the silence. The siren continued until it stopped outside the house.

"Fire department!" a voice called from the front of the house.

"In here!" Dupree responded.

The sound of heavy footsteps and clattering gear came down the hall.

"Sweet Jesus, what happened here?" A tall graying fireman said from the door. "Is that Dara Walker?"

Dupree nodded. "She's really hurt."

"We got this. Please let me have a look." Dupree softly laid Dara down. It was then he realized she passed out.

Dupree moved out of the way. "What the hell happened to her? I just got here, we were supposed to have dinner. The front door was wide open."

"An ambulance is on its way, but it's going to take a few minutes," the fireman said, reassuring him.

"Just do what you can, please."

"I need oxygen and morphine. We need to get her stabilized, her blood pressure is really low," the fireman said, taking off the blood pressure cuff.

The two firemen worked quickly and efficiently. The first one through the door spoke gently and with affection to Dara. "Dara, it's Ryan Jacobs. You've been hurt pretty bad, but you're going to be okay. Don't worry, you're family, we're not letting anything happen to you, sweetheart. Don't you worry."

Dupree got the impression the fireman was talking as much for his own sake as Dara's.

The man standing with Dupree whispered softly, "Ryan was Mitch Walker's best friend. Best man, you name it, they went all the way back to kindergarten."

"Then she's in good hands," Dupree said softly.

It took nearly twenty minutes for the ambulance to arrive.

A pair of young paramedics loaded Dara onto a gurney and moved her to the ambulance. Dupree closed the front door, then climbed into the back of the ambulance with Dara as they began the long ride to the hospital.

1325 Confidence Street was owned by Nancy Polanski. She spent most of her time in Vancouver. She owned an art gallery on the water that was a favorite of tourists from the cruise ships. The cottage in White Owl was purchased by her late husband. Nancy cared little about the house. She came for Festival weekends, but other than that the house sat empty. She paid local gardeners, painters, carpenters, a house cleaner, and Kenny Perry to repeatedly work on the house. The guilt she felt at the hard time she gave her husband about buying a second house was somehow eased by paying for maintenance. Work that really didn't need to be done.

The sight of workers coming and going was so common that the neighbors paid no attention when Kenny's Septic Tank Service arrived for another visit. The visits were usually done bi-monthly and after hours, to not interfere with customers who actually needed service. Kenny pulled his truck around the side of the fenceless property. Large pines formed a thick barrier between the cottage and its neighbors.

Kenny turned off his light so as to not draw any more attention than necessary. The system was on an automatic water feed. The levels were maintained so that when Nancy Polanski paid a visit she didn't fear system failure. The idea that a septic tank needed to be half full and serviced every other month was ridiculous to Kenny, but the twelve hundred dollars a year additional income was no laughing matter. He followed the owner's orders with a smile.

The tank opening was at the back of the large lot. Kenny backed up the truck to the large cement cover. Using the same crowbar he used on Slader, he removed the lid. He glanced in the opening. He flashed a beam of light into the tank. Water reflected in the light. Kenny dropped the crowbar into the tank.

As quickly as Slader's dead weight would allow, he dragged his body from the truck to the opening of the septic tank. For a fleeting moment, Kenny thought of a burial at sea. He shoved Deputy Travis Slader's body into the darkness of the septic tank.

"He came from shit, and to shit he returns." Kenny mocked.

Returning to the truck, he took three one-gallon jugs from the storage space opposite where Slader was stowed. He quickly uncapped the jugs. Bio-Pig Crud Eater was an enzyme solution designed to turn organic waste and paper from toilets and sinks into a creamy liquid that would easily and safely run from the tank's leach lines into the soil and be eco-friendly. In a tank this size, a jug per year would chomp its way through waste no matter how solid or impacted it was.

Kenny poured the contents of all three jugs into the tank and dropped them in behind. "That should eat up ol' Travis in a week." Kenny's sense of satisfaction at the eradication of his lifelong nemesis was reaching nearly hysterical levels. He moved the lid back onto the tank and stomped hard.

"See you in two months," Kenny said with a wide grin.

It was nearly three hours before Dara was placed in her room in the hospital. She underwent numerous tests, MRIs and various x-rays and scans. Her face was wrapped and bandaged. She was breathing with an oxygen mask, and several IVs were feeding her medications and fluids.

An Indian doctor was assigned to Dara's treatment, and he paid a visit to her once she was settled. Dupree greeted him and introduced himself as Dara's lawyer.

"She is a tough girl, Mr. Dupree. This kind of beating would have killed a lesser woman. She has sustained, as you know, serious trauma to the face, all of which will heal in time. There is some swelling of the brain and we will be watching that closely. Time, rest, and support from loved ones will get her through. The swelling, which I must admit is pretty grotesque at this point, should begin to go down in a few days. We have stitched her mouth wounds from the inside and they should not even be noticeable in a month or so. The other wounds are not deep and will also heal without scarring. The internal injuries to her pelvic region are not severe. A bit of tearing, this is common in these cases. Do you have any questions?"

"How long until she will be able to go home?"

"If the swelling to her brain is not significant and it shrinks as I hope it will, four or five days. In the meantime, her mental state is of concern. Please notify her family as soon as possible. It is going to take a lot of love and handholding."

"Thank you, doctor."

Sometime around midnight, Dupree fell asleep holding Dara's hand. The comings and goings of nurses through the night woke Dupree repeatedly. When they left, he would take Dara's hand in his again, rest his head on the bed next to her, and fall asleep.

"You awake?"

Dupree opened one eye and saw Burt Carr standing by the side of the bed.

"Yeah, what time is it?"

"Little after seven. I figured I would be back here, but not this quick. How's she doing?"

"Thankfully, it looks far worse than the actual damage. It will take time but she's going to be alright."

"Sorry I ducked out on you the other day. I figured you were going to drag me to a doctor and made a break for it." Carr gave Dupree a sheepish grin. "Let's talk outside."

The two men went into the hallway. A young woman in white, standing by the nurses' station, pantomimed drinking coffee and gave Dupree an inquisitive nod. Dupree raised two fingers.

"I'm really sorry about Dara. I got here as soon as I could. We'll get whoever did this." Carr began. "It seems Slader didn't, or hasn't, reported for duty. I drove over to Dara's, it doesn't appear anyone has been there."

"We left around seven-thirty."

"Here's the thing. Slader's black Camaro is parked up the block. I have an APB out on Slader, but without him being in his own car, well..."

"It's him, Carr."

"We'll get him." There was no questioning Carr's statement.

The week passed, Dara improved greatly, the fear of brain swelling proved to be without merit. Though still badly bruised, the swelling in Dara's eyes and lips reduced by half and she was able to drink through a straw. Best of all, she was able to talk, albeit, thick and difficult to understand at times. She was alert and able to chat with Dupree. They spent most of the afternoons each day holding hands and enjoying each other's company.

Burt Carr had left after two days. The rape kit and examination samples provided DNA positively matching Slader. Slader's car was impounded by the State Police, and door to door interviews were done on both sides of the street for two blocks around Dara's house.

Kenny Perry's wife explained to the officer conducting the interview while holding a screaming baby in her arms that her family was in Seattle on the date in question. The child's kicking and screaming caused her to unintentionally forget to mention that Kenny stayed home. Her responses seemed to satisfy the investigator, who was more than happy to leave the wailing child behind the closing door. The Perry house was the last on his list, and he made his way back to his car with a notebook full of nothing.

After seven days there was still no sign of Slader. His wallet was found in the car, credit cards and cash intact. His bank account was put under close watch and his assets frozen. Travis Slader, as far as the police were concerned, simply vanished.

Dupree spent as much time as he could at Dara's side. Burt Carr gave him a ride to Dara's house before he left town, and Dupree was able to find her keys, lock the front door, and borrow her car.

On the sixth day, the doctor released Dara. With list in hand the night prior, Dupree returned to Dara's house and collected various items. She went from the hospital back home in the passenger seat beside Dupree. For most of the drive, she rested her head on his shoulder.

"Whose car is that?" Dara asked, pointing to a small car at the curb as they pulled into her drive.

"It's a surprise."

"Oh, please Adam, I can't see anybody looking like this."

"Just trust me. You'll be pleased, I promise." Dupree jumped out of the car and moved around to open Dara's door.

Arm in arm, they carefully mounted the steps. "You're sure you're okay with this?" Dupree asked.

"This is my home. I will not be driven out by a memory," she replied in a fierce voice just above a whisper.

"Damn the torpedoes, full steam ahead!" Dupree said jovially.

Dupree unlocked the front door and they stepped inside.

"Hi, Dara!" A slim young woman in a baby blue uniform smiled and gave Dara an excited wave from the middle of the living room.

"Bonnie! What are you doing here?"

"Your wonderful boyfriend there said you could use a day at the spa, but would never agree to go. So, the spa has come to you! Right this way, Madame." Bonnie bowed and with a wave of her arm directed Dara into the kitchen.

Sitting at the kitchen sink was an elevated chair out of Bonnie's beauty parlor. "First a shampoo and haircut. My assistant will be here shortly for your pedicure and manicure. After that, we have a masseuse lined up for a head-to-toe full body massage. And now you, sir, are dismissed to go about your duties."

"You must be all done by five o'clock because that's when the caterer arrives."

"Let me worry about the time. You be back at the agreed time, and everything will be fine." Bonnie gave Dupree a big smile and a dismissive gesture with her hand.

"You heard the lady, this is girl time." Dara's voice chimed with her delight at Dupree's thoughtful gift. "Oh, and Adam."

"Yes," Dupree turned expecting a request.

"I love you." Dara blew him a kiss from her bruised and still swollen lips.

Dupree walked to his office, counting his blessings. Through the pain and heartbreak of the attack, he realized the most important thing in his life was to do everything he could to spend the rest of his days taking care of Dara. He put on a brave face, but in quiet moments Dupree could see beyond the swelling and see the pain in her eyes.

He would live in White Owl, he would marry Dara Walker if she would have him, and they would grow old together, an example to anyone who had eyes that love is the greatest healer of all.

Epilogue

The little cottage at 1325 Confidence Street owned by Nancy Polanski was sold to a young couple who came to teach at the new elementary school. The inspector said that for a seventy-year-old home, it was as close to perfect as he ever saw.

Along the bluff, above the river on the east side of town, a small subdivision was built and advertised using an image very similar to the white owl in the Harry Potter movies. Millennials, raised on the magical stories, were sure that something wonderful was possible in White Owl.

The draw of high paying jobs at the new Internet communication center drew hundreds of applicants looking to escape the frantic pace of Seattle. Suddenly joggers, bikers, and moms pushing strollers were seen on the streets and the newly built river park trail in White Owl.

A senior citizen retirement community was built overlooking the river. Three hundred active seniors came to White Owl with their electric scooters and social security checks. They welcomed the community to weekly movie nights and monthly craft fairs. Mrs. Curtis' third-grade class was brought once a week to visit a senior as part of the Adopt a Grandparent program.

The changes brought new life and vitality to the once sleepy little town. New businesses, and renewed established ones, served the needs of all the new residences. The older timers, as they were now called, viewed the changes with mixed feelings.

Pete Olson expanded his inventory to include a variety of computer cords, hard drives, and supplies for printers, accessories for cell phones, and tablets of all kinds.

Tyler Franz expanded his brewery to include a visitor's center, hourly tours on weekends, complete with beer sampling, barbecued ribs, and hamburgers. T-shirts were sold by the dozens with the White Owl Brewery and Pub logo emblazoned across the chest.

At the center of the increased demand for Foodies fare was The Quarter Moon Café. The selection of the breads and loaves locals loved for years seemed to be way ahead of the curve. A variety of fresh brewed lattes, cappuccinos, and espressos added to the draw for the new wave of Owlies, as they called themselves. The breakfast menu expanded with the additions of egg white omelets, granola, and a selection of vegan options. The new offerings were made fun of by some of the old-timers but their bacon, eggs, and hash browns were still available in abundance, so they calmed down after a week or two.

Lunch became a hotspot for executives from the communication center, who rode their Segways up Opportunity Street and parked in front of The Quarter Moon. They munched on salads and artisan personalized pizzas. They drank gallons of Dara's iced green tea.

The biggest change to The Quarter Moon was the addition of dinner. A young energetic chef from Seattle followed his partner to White Owl when he was hired by the Communication Center. Without work and showing signs of cabin fever, Swain Robbins approached Dara with the idea of partnering up on an evening schedule. The idea was all organic, local produce, Chef's Choice menu. Each night Swain offered a full course dinner of a variety never seen in this part of the state. Trout, elk, wild turkey, were all offered along with vegan salad buffets, homemade pastas, and cook-it-yourself steak night. From the first week, it was a hit.

The changes weren't all good. The White Owl Summer Solstice Music and Art Festival was no longer the boon to the town it once was. The influx of drug-fueled crazies and drunken hooligans were met with open hostility by the city council. The increased number of problems brought a rash of complaints from the merchants and vendors at the now-famous street fair.

When Mike Kelly and Teddy Auckland came to the council with their plan to sell the festival, the council voted unanimously to revoke all future permits for outdoor music festivals. The Street Fair could stay but the Festival would have to go. Kelly and Auckland turned over their interest in the Street Fair to Carl and Cathy Walker. The era of flowers, patchouli, and tie-dye had come to an end. Arts, crafts, antiques, and booth after booth of cheeses, homemade salsas, jams, jellies, and organic cookies were now the annual draw to White Owl.

The familiar faces of White Owl began to disappear as well. Grammy Morrow had a stroke and died shortly after. Marsh Peterson retired and moved to Wisconsin to be near his sister.

The Whartons divorced shortly after Toby's arrest for 'setting the fire' at The Quarter Moon. The charges were dropped when Dupree testified Slader's report was inaccurate, and possibly intentionally falsified to cover his own actions. Burt Carr filed a damning report on the corruption in the Sheriff's office and the sheriff resigned, Slader's uncle was convicted of multiple counts of falsifying records, graft, and criminal activity tied to a local drug dealer.

Jack Wharton left town after the divorce. No one is quite sure what happened to him, but it was rumored he opened a small bookkeeping office in Kirkland. The furniture store received a complete makeover. Home furnishings more in keeping with the new arrivals now filled the showroom. The dark, dimly lit store was painted bright white. Industrial style lighting and colorful splashes of colorful artwork created an atmosphere of playful excitement.

Toby Wharton eventually was able to become a 'Bust Boy,' but the results were less than stellar. After a week of clearing tables, broken dishes, tears, and frustration, Toby was allowed to do the job that suited him the most, Dishwasher. He loved the steam, water, and sound of the massive dishwasher machine. He seemed to have a real knack for stacking and sorting the clean dishes and flatware. He was always early and always stayed late. The wait staff loved him. The newest busboy split part of his tips with Toby because Toby made his job so easy.

Robin Epperson returned to White Owl as an RN. The new clinic was a perfect fit for the White Owl native. The house she shared with Jeremy was partially burned in a fire and was rebuilt, remodeled, and available. She and her children moved into a new home with none of the memories connected with the old structure. Jeremy met with several violent incidents in prison. As was his life's pattern, his mouth got him in trouble with a group of Mexican gangsters who took offense at his comments in the yard.

After a vicious attack landed him in the prison hospital, he vowed revenge. On his way to his table in the mess hall a short while later, he shoved a sharpened toothbrush into the eye of a member of the group who attacked him. The force of the blow thrust the plastic weapon into the brain of his victim, killing him instantly. Jeremy received a life sentence for first-degree murder with gang enhancement and was moved to a maximum-security prison for his own safety.

The men who worked in the building trades and survived the downtimes found themselves with more work than they knew how to schedule: remodeling, custom touches to the subdivision homes, and facelifts for existing buildings and stores. Three of the old-timers pooled their resources and bought an Ace Hardware franchise. The boom in White Owl created jobs for young and old alike.

Dara met a group from the Communication Center whom she overheard complaining about legal representation for their various expansion projects. With that chance piece of the conversation, Dupree was introduced to the corporate side of the exploding start-up. He readily became the chief legal counsel for Ecomm Quantum, Inc. Within six months he was invited to take up residence in their executive offices. It was the best of all possible worlds, the kind of law he loved and none of the restrictions and worries of his own practice. He maintained the office above Olson's for his active community pro bono program.

    Sometime during the growth years, Terry and the twins had a falling out. The whole town knew they argued and caused a scene in front of The Quarter Moon. Oddly, no one could really tell what caused the rift in the lifelong friends. The hurt was deep, pride was shattered, and egos bruised. Taking the first step to a reconciliation was not a possibility for either side. The brothers were committed to each other, no matter what they felt or believed. One cold winter night Terry packed up a U-Haul truck and he and his family left town.

    It wasn't long after that Cal got an offer of a job in the oil fields of North Dakota. Upon his arrival, he called his brother and asked him if he would like a job in the company Cal found himself managing. Past hard feelings about the family business were buried and forgiven. Kenny sold the business to a kid who worked for him part-time. The terms were good and the young man made money from the start. Kenny, his wife, and kids left for Dakota a month later. The faces of the trio and their rambunctious conversation left a void in the morning make-up of The Quarter

Moon. Time tends to erase memories, and the new clientele was unaware of the disappearance, one by one, of the old guard.

The night before Kenny's family left town he drove over to 1325 Confidence Street. The sun was setting and the couple who bought the place was in the front yard putting the finishing touches on their new flower beds. Kenny got out of the car and approached them.

"Afternoon!" Kenny said cheerfully. "My name is Perry, Kenny Perry. I used to live here when I was a kid. I was wondering," he paused, trying to figure out how to complete the deception. "Could I take a look at the back yard? I spent a lot of great times back there. We're leaving town tomorrow and I kind of wanted to have one last look."

"I think that's sweet," said the young woman with the ponytail, muddy knees, and thick glasses.

"Help yourself, were just finishing up here," her husband offered, not looking up.

"My mom would have loved it." Kenny waved his arm across the yard as another layer of falsehood. Moving at a leisurely pace, Kenny strolled around the corner of the house. Then with long strides and a guilty heart he made his way to the back of the lot. The new owner's makeover of the backyard included a tall redwood fence across the back of the property. The concrete lid to the septic tank was surrounded by a short white picket fence. The lid was painted to look like a door. A small sign reading, Go Away! Occupant Sleeping hung from the doorknob.

Kenny laughed out loud and said, "I'll be damned." On his way back to the car, Kenny waved to the new owners, "Looks beautiful. I love what you've done with the place."

They waved and thanked him, and never gave the stranger and his sentimental request another thought.

Dara fully recovered from her wounds and bruises of Slader's attack. Inside was a different story. She often woke in the night in terror. She became fanatical about doors and windows being triple checked at night. Dupree insisted that she receive treatment from the psychiatrist at the hospital. With a lot of work, Dupree's understanding, and the careful guidance of the Doctor, Dara slowly began to return to her pre-rape self.

The emotional scars took their toll on the relationship between Dara and Dupree as well. What began as a deep connection, hours of handholding, and hugs on the couch, several months later turned to complete rejection of physical touch. The psychiatrist told Dupree privately that it was part of the healing cycle and to show his love in different ways until she worked through the physical hurdle of healing.

While taking an evening walk, Dara reached over and took Dupree's hand. It became a nightly ritual until, when he delivered her to her door, she took his face in her hands and kissed him.

"I know this has been hard for you. A lesser man would have left a nutcase like me two years ago. I know I haven't said it since I went home from the hospital, but, Adam I love you more than anything on earth. Can you forgive me?"

"Shhh," he said, "There is nothing to forgive. If it takes another ten years I am here for you. I will be here as long as you want me."

"Forever should be about right then." Dara kissed him again and wrapped her arms around his neck.

At dinner a week later, Dupree asked Dara to marry him. He gave her his mother's engagement ring. "This ring is a symbol of the strength of the two women I have loved most in my life. Whatever life brings or wherever it takes us, whatever joy or pain that may come, I will love you without question and ask nothing in return. Dara, you have become my life. Will you marry me?"

"Thank you for waiting. I know I have been difficult at times. For that, I ask your forgiveness. I can think of nothing that would give me more happiness than to become your wife."

They were married three months later. TJ, though nearly eight months pregnant, was Dara's maid of honor. Her husband, an information tech at the Communication Center stood by just in case, with a suitcase ready for the hospital. TJ insisted it wasn't necessary but secretly was delighted at the attention. Martin Hutchinson came from L.A. with his wife Chrissie and stood as Dupree's best man.

Dupree, in an olive branch last try at reaching his children, sent them both an invitation. Deanna returned the invitation with a nasty, "Hell No!" and signed Rene scrawled across the RSVP card. Dara asked Dupree who it was and he just laughed and said, "Someone I used to know."

The biggest surprise of their special day came when a handsome, dark-haired young man in a tie, brown leather jacket, and chinos came through the back door of the church. On his arm was a beautiful Asian woman with long black hair, and a proud, yet mischievous, smile on her face. The ceremony hadn't started, but Dupree and Hutchinson were standing in the front of the church.

Without saying a word, Dupree ran from the platform to the middle of the aisle where the couple was making their way to a seat on the groom's side. Dupree threw his arms around the young man and gave him a bear hug.

"Thank you, son, thank you!" Dupree said, with tears streaming down his cheeks. "Ladies and Gentlemen, I want you to all meet my son, Eric!"

The congregation burst into applause. Eric's date gave Dupree a hug, kissed him on the cheek, and whispered, "Thank you! I'm Amy."

As Dupree retook his place, the organ began Here Comes the Bride and Dara and Carl Walker began their stroll down the aisle. Dara was dressed in a beautiful, off-white lace dress and a single string of pearls. Though it wasn't a bridal gown, there wasn't anyone in attendance who would not have agreed she was one of the loveliest brides they ever saw.

At the reception held at The Quarter Moon, many friends, old and new, greeted the bride and groom. To help control her nerves, Dara baked her own wedding cake. To Dupree's delight, the bottom layer was chocolate zucchini. The second layer was banana nut, and the top chocolate chip banana nut. The frosting was Dara's famous cream cheese recipe. Swain and the evening staff acted as servers and dressed in white tuxedo shirts and black vests. Swain bought all the servers the gift of a quarter moon rhinestone broach for the occasion and signed Dara's name.

After a quick sweep of the café, Dupree realized that Eric was not there. His heart sank. He made various excuses to himself; he embarrassed him, he couldn't face Dupree, the girl wanted to leave, they went to buy a gift, but they all rang hollow. He saw him. He looked well, the girlfriend was beautiful and he seemed happy. She thanked Dupree in the church. He would hold onto that and cherish it. That would have to be enough.

In all the excitement, Dupree didn't see two very special guests until the wedding party was seated for at least ten minutes. To his surprise, sitting along the windows and near the back were Chet and Valericia Weaver. Next to them sat a young man in a crisp new western shirt.

Excusing himself, Dupree made his way across the room. Pausing only for good wishes and high fives, he made his way to where the Weavers sat. Valericia stood first and met Dupree next to the table.

"God's answered my prayers and blessed you as he blessed us with you." They hugged, and Valericia gave Dupree a kiss on the cheek. "Here, you muss meet someone!"

The young man stood and extended his hand to Dupree. "This is our Tucker, newest memmer of the Dean's List at UC Davis." Valericia's face beamed with pride.

"Hello, Mr. Dupree, I don't know quite how to say how much you have done for us. Thank you. My parents send thanks as well."

"I was, and am, thrilled to see that it is going to make your grandparents' dreams come true for you. I hope you understand what a lucky young man you are." Dupree patted Tucker on the shoulder. "I know you won't let them down."

"No sir, never."

Chet weaver stood and faced Dupree. "You're kind of pretty without those raccoon black eyes I last saw you with." The group laughed.

"You have no idea how thrilled I am to have you here. This truly has made my day."

"We are nothing compared to seeing your son. Wha' a handsome young man. Did you know he was coming? " Valericia inquired.

"No, it was a complete shock to me. I sent the invitation as a way of letting him know what I was doing in my life. I didn't even have an address. My friend Marty, my best man, got it to him somehow," Dupree said with a melancholy smile.

"I would love to meet him. Where is he?" Valericia inquired.

"I don't know. They haven't arrived yet."

Valericia reached out and took Dupree's hand. "It will be alright, you'll see. God got 'im this far, he's not going to let you down now. I'll say a prayer."

"You do that. Dara doesn't even know he came."

"You better get back to your beautiful bride!" Chet said cheerfully.

"I hope you're sticking around for a day or two. I want Dara to meet you all. I've told her all about you."

"Yep, we're here for the weekend. But, what about your honeymoon?"

"Next week. I'm taking Dara to Ireland, she's always wanted to go there."

"We are at the little motel as you come into town, room 213. We'll catch up. I think somebody is looking for you," Chet said, pointing toward the door.

His leather jacket and tie were gone, Eric smiled as he met Dupree's eyes. Amy wore a pair of gray slacks and a ruby red blouse instead of the black dress she wore to the ceremony. They both looked more relaxed, casual, and comfortable.

Dupree reached up and undid his bowtie. He waved and began making his way to the front door.

"Sorry we're late. I just had to get out of that hangman's noose," Eric shrugged.

"Me too." Dupree held up the bow tie as he undid his top button. "Come here, there's someone I want you to meet." He didn't make anyone suffer any awkward silence.

"Sweetheart, this is my son, Eric."

Dara stood and, with tears welling in her eyes, threw her arms around Eric and gave him a long hug. She smiled at Amy and gave her a welcoming hug. "I am so glad to meet you. Thank you for coming. You have made our special day even better. Please sit with us."

"Hi, Eric. Glad you made it." Dupree grinned.

"Hi. Let me introduce my fiancé, Amy."

"Well, Amy that is an excuse for another hug." Dupree smiled and spread his arms. Without hesitancy, Amy embraced her father-in-law to be. "Can this day get any better?" he asked as they separated.

"You know Chrissie," Dupree said, indicating Martin Hutchinson's wife.

"Of course, how are you?" Eric smiled broadly and moved toward the two chairs Swain brought to the head table. The couple was seated across from Dara and Dupree. In Dupree's mind, the rest of the room just disappeared. He looked at Eric for a long moment. The unkempt mess he saw his last day in L.A. was now a well-groomed, tanned, toned adult. The young woman beside him watched Dupree closely. When their eyes met, she smiled at him with reassurance and affection.

"Tell, tell," Dara began excitedly, "where did you meet? How did he propose? Have you set a date?"

"See what I'm in for?" Dupree injected.

"Well, we met at church."

"Church?" Dupree asked, trying to hide his astonishment.

"Yeah, I'm on staff. I work most of the week as a secretary but I also work with Eric in the high school group."

"High school group?" Dupree could no longer cover his shock at what he was hearing.

"Maybe it should be my turn," Eric cut in. "The day you took off was a life-changing day for both of us. That afternoon I was swept up in a drug bust. Thankfully, I wasn't in possession of anything. The judge, and God, were merciful to me and he gave me the choice of jail or rehab." Eric looked for a long moment at his father. "Yeah, I was pretty bad off. You would never have known because you spent as little time at home as I did and probably for the same reasons."

"I never..." Dupree choked up.

"It's okay Dad, it was part of the plan. I went to Vista, down by San Diego. There was a facility that I figured I could bluff my way out of. Wrong." Eric chuckled. "I got down there and they were buying nothing I was trying to sell. We were required to attend chapel once a week. They had a bunch of different kinds, Catholic, Jewish, even a new age spiritual kind of thing. Anyway, I went to the one they called non-denominational Christian."

"Any reason?" Dara asked.

"I remembered Dad saying his mom was a Christian, on Christmas once. One of the few times at our house that the reason for the season was ever mentioned. So this guy named Chris Brown, in a t-shirt, jeans, and flip flops, spoke."

"He's my boss." Amy grinned.

"He talked about God like he knew him. It was really weird. Then he said, your life isn't shot to hell, hell has shot up your life. I started crying. I don't know why, well I do now, but I bawled like a baby. When we were dismissed I just sat there. Chris came over and told me about how God had changed his life, and I said that my life really needed changing. He kind of took me under his wing. I prayed to accept Christ that day, and he stuck with me until I got out of rehab."

"This is the part I like!" Amy chimed in.

"He gave me a job on staff."

"As a preacher?" Dupree asked.

"No, no as a janitor! I washed toilets, wiped baby puke up off the nursery carpet, cleaned windows, dumped trash, and vacuumed the entire Costco sized building. That's when I met Amy. She kept my time card. Morning, lunch, and quitting time, I got to see her."

"I thought he was pretty cute, but Chris said to be careful. He was 'new in his walk and just got out of rehab, so give him room to grow. He doesn't need romantic entanglement right now'."

"Sounds like a smart guy," Dara interjected.

"Anyway, a year later I started working in the high school group on Wednesday nights. I even played guitar! Can you believe it? In front of people! One thing led to another and when the high school leader moved to another campus, Chris asked me if I wanted the job."

"I don't think I know what to say," Dupree said in amazement.

"Say something nice," Amy warned with a smile. "He was scared you wouldn't like it."

"I'm thrilled. It's wonderful. I'm so proud of you, I just can't put it in words."

"You mean, you could have married us?" Dara asked.

"No, I'm not ordained or anything, I'm still going to seminary."

"Why didn't you tell me any of this, Marty?" Dupree turned to his best man with his hands out palms up.

"What, and spoil missing the look on your face?" Hutchinson asked happily.

"We pray for you all the time," Amy said. "We didn't know where you were or what you were doing, but we just prayed God would bring you peace in your spirit and make you happy."

"Count that prayer answered," he said, taking Dara's hand.

"Okay, we know how you met, what about the proposal?"

"My turn." Amy patted Eric on the arm. "After church on Sunday, I went out to my car and there was a red balloon on about a ten-foot ribbon tied to my bumper. There was a note inside the balloon, so I had to pop it. 'Come to the palm trees,' it read. So I went back to the middle of the square in front of the building and there was a note tacked to the tree. 'Meet me at staff parking.' When I got there, he was standing by this orange Porsche that a church member loaned him.

"We drove to a park with a beautiful lake, and this silly guy pulls right up onto the lawn and to a table which was set and waiting by the water! We had a waiter all ready to serve us lunch. The first thing he brought was barbecued oysters in the shell. Now, being Japanese, we eat a lot of shellfish, but there was something strange about the one I was served. Eric popped his open and ate it. I was struggling to get mine open. It was like it was glued shut. When it finally popped open, there was a diamond ring and a note that said, Will you be mine?" The group applauded and there were compliments all around when Amy showed off her ring.

When the guests began to leave, there were lots of hugs and pats on the back and more good wishes. When the last guest was out the door, Dara locked it and they sat at the front table and talked for several hours. Eric, Marty, and Dupree went to the kitchen twice for leftovers. Swain and the staff came out after a couple of hours and wished Dara and Dupree well, and took their leave.

As the sun set the conversation began to lag, so Marty and Chrissie left for the motel. Dupree didn't want the time with Eric to end but knew he couldn't hold them much longer. Finally, Amy gracefully said they probably should let the newlyweds have some alone time.

Eric stood and gave his father a big hug. "I hope this is the start of a new life for us together. If you can, I sincerely pray that you can find it in your heart to forgive me for any hurt I have caused you. I know you were as disappointed in me as I was in myself. I love you, Dad."

"I love you too." Dupree could barely speak for the lump in his throat. "I am so proud of the man you have become. I am ashamed of the years I neglected you. I hope you can forgive me as well." Tears were streaming down both of their cheeks. They embraced again.

When they released each other, Dupree turned to look at Dara. She and Amy were both crying. And smiling.

The next day Dara cooked a huge spaghetti and meatball lunch, and Dupree grilled Italian sausages. Dupree asked Eric to bless the food. The Weavers, Hutchinsons, Burt Carr, and Eric and Amy all stayed until late in the evening. When they parted, there were promises of return visits, and all the women vowed to help Amy any way they could with the wedding.

When Eric and Amy walked down the sidewalk to their car, Dupree took Dara's hand and said, "If I ever doubted the existence of God, today took care of that forever. There has to be a God because my life is a miracle."

"I never doubted. I know there is a God because he answered my prayers when He sent me you."

The sun came through the swaying trees and created a strobe light effect on the bedroom wall. Dara lay warm and asleep next to him. Her soft breathing and slightly stale breath brought a smile to Dupree. He reached up and gently moved the hair from her face. The white forelock, that he loved so, seemed to have more company each day. The gray was becoming; after all, he thought she earned them. The strength of the woman he loved was a constant source of inspiration to Dupree. The difference that only he saw in her was hidden from the world by her dazzling smile and warm, inclusive personality.

But he knew the pain that still would flash across her eyes when she was standing alone, unaware she was being adored from a distance. For fleeting moments that grew farther apart as the days and months passed, Dupree saw a deep hurt, fear, and anger that the rest of the world never saw. He kissed his fingertips and softly transferred them to her forehead.

He was content for the first time in his life. He loved his work, he adored the woman beside him, their life together, and the home she opened to him. He thought of Eric and Amy and breathed a prayer that their life would be different than his. He thanked God for the opportunity to build a meaningful relationship with his son. If somehow Deanna could have a change of heart, that would be a miracle indeed. He wouldn't expect or dwell on it.

His happiness would not be built on regrets of the past. The promise of tomorrow was not guaranteed. The actions of others were out of his control, and he was learning to see that the pain he caused others would be dealt with, forgiveness would be asked, if and when he was given the chance.

Across his thoughts, he saw the face of the stoner, Cutter, who picked him up on the way north. Dupree reached up and felt the bridge of his nose, the tiny scar, and the slight bump in the cartilage. He, without knowing or caring, changed the trajectory of Dupree's life. The people he met, the revelations about the law that came helping the Weavers, and the humbling that the black eyes brought him, were all part of the grand scheme of his life. He smiled.

Dupree took a deep breath and recalled the words of Robert Browning, *God is in His heaven, and all is right with the world.* And it was.

THE END

DUPREE'S RESOLVE

Exclusive sample from Book 3

Chapter One

"Good morning! You're up early for a Friday Morning."

"I have to get up early if I'm going to see you." Dupree smiled giving Dara a peck on the cheek.

"So, what's on your agenda for this lovely morning?" Dara turned to face him.

"I'm not quite sure. There is a whole new vibe with the new staff. The buy-out has left a lot of our staff jittery. I've seen at least a dozen people who are scared to death they are going to be replaced or made redundant by the new automated systems that are being installed." Dupree reached for the lid of the pan on the stove Dara was using.

"What's your read on these new guys?" Dara reached over and gently pushed his shoulder. "No peeking."

"I hate 'em."

"Gee, don't hold back."

"They are, for the most part, smug, arrogant, newly rich, condescending punks. That's my legal opinion." Dupree laughed heartily.

"Well, it's good to see you aren't letting your personal feelings cloud your judgment." Dara slapped him on the butt as she passed him. "Come for lunch? Hot turkey sandwich, your fav is the special."

"I'll be there."

Two pieces of sourdough bread popped up from the toaster. Dara spread peanut butter on one and cream cheese on the other.

"Bacon?" She folded back the paper towel covering the breakfast surprise.

"Please."

Dara put two thick strips of bacon on the peanut buttered toast. "Black coffee, Butter 'n' Bacon on sourdough, up for table one."

Breakfast was over and Dara was on her way to the Café. Dupree sat drinking his second cup of coffee. He felt a bit guilty for not telling Dara what was really going on at the Center.

Ecomm Quantrum, Inc. was the brainchild of two UC Berkeley computer geeks, Cameron Bartram and Joshua Stanton. Their idea was to develop a system to network and funnel text, email, Teletypewriter, or TTY, for the deaf into a one-stop communication center that used a platform they designed. Ecomm's software revolutionized the speed and size of messaging being transported over the internet.

This whole process was a threat to all the giants of internet technology. After graduation, and several successful years working and growing their business in the Bay Area, it was decided a move to the northwest, the most desirable place for the founders and their loyal followers to work and live. For a year, it was a utopian dream.

White Owl was a perfect fit. The company was eco-friendly, community-focused, and all was right with the world. But, it seems they were becoming too successful. Microsoft decided to sue Bartram and Stanton for unfair trade practices, and a deeply veiled threat of copyright infringement. The cost of fighting one of the world's richest companies along with their whisper campaign inferring the company was soon to be insolvent, was too much.

That's when a conglomerate of young, startup millionaires made a sizable offer to Bartram and Stanton. News travels fast in the computer world and their offer was followed by an even better one from a company in Europe. As Stanton told Dupree in a closed-door meeting, "We didn't sign up for this kind of aggravation." They took their money and rode off into the sunset, Bartram bought a boat and sailed the Pacific. Stanton bought a ranch in Montana

The company was purchased by a Dutch conglomerate, and re-named Kanaal Communications, to match their European Social Media and Tele-Communications empire. The new administration was transferred in from a cannibalized take-over in California. It made a bunch of Silicon Valley wannabes into millionaires, with inflated egos to match. They removed the offending elements of the Ecomm process and sold Microsoft the software for somewhere in the low seven figures, a figure Dupree was not privy to.

The things that made Ecomm a great place to work were, not all that slowly, being done away with. The new owners brought in a lot of their own people. This was not unusual or unexpected. What was problematic was their unwillingness to fit in with the Ecomm family. The new staff were young, single, overpaid and friends of the new management. They thought they were above rules, policies, and proper behavior.

Like the rest of the employees. Dupree went with the sale. For a while, it was business as usual. The threat of litigation by Microsoft and other giant tech companies was dissolved with the sale. Dupree wrote contracts, settled disputes, and advised on employee conflicts.

That is where Dupree found himself between the devil and his better angels. Daily since the takeover, employee after employee made their way to his office seeking advice and protection from termination. Though there was never a formal arrangement with Bartram and Stanton, Dupree was the attorney for the company, and as such was bound to protect and defend the company assets.

The feeling in the building was just not the same anymore. As Dupree went through the security gate, the guard didn't smile or greet him. The usually friendly man in the blue uniform seemed sullen and distant. Much of the art was removed from the lobby and the halls of the building. It was those bright splashes of abstract and pop art that were part of the constant stimulation that gave Ecomm its positive, engaging atmosphere. More than that, though, the spirit of the company seemed to be sucked out of the building, along with the hearts of the employees.

"Good Morning, Mr. Dupree." Dupree's secretary would have made a good funeral attendant.

"Morning Melinda!" Dupree tried to respond to her gloom with a cheerful smile.

"There's a Tomara French in your office."

Dupree glanced over to the closed door and darkened panel of ribbed glass alongside it.

"She said she was afraid to sit out here, so I let her go in. She turned off the lights. Hope you don't mind."

"No, no, it's fine," Dupree moved toward the door. "Good Morning," Dupree went into his office and flicked on the lights.

"I'm sorry to have…" The pretty young woman with a little redder than auburn hair began.

"No, it's fine. Are you alright? Physically, I mean."

"Yes. I need someone to talk to I can trust. People around here speak highly of you."

Dupree approached where the young woman sat and extended his hand. "I'm Dupree, I guess you know I'm the company's legal counsel."

"I'm Tomara, people usually call me Tomi." She took his hand and squeezed it like she was clutching the rope's end that kept her from falling into the abyss.

Taking the chair behind his desk, Dupree smiled and tried to get a read on the emotional state of the young woman. Her eyes were a bit swollen and red from crying.

"I came straight here from HR." She sat a little straighter. "They tried to give me money. Can you imagine?" Tomi's anger got the better of her and she burst into tears.

"I can see you're upset. Take a deep breath and let's start at the beginning. Were you let go?"

"I wish!" Tomi burst into tears. Dupree sensed an innocence, or an underlying sweetness, to Tomi. He was finding it hard to judge her age, but he knew she was well under twenty-five.

Dupree grabbed a box of tissues from the credenza behind him and pushed it across the desk. He sat silently while the young woman tried to pull herself together.

She took a deep breath and began again. "I went to HR to report sexual harassment. They offered me money to keep quiet. They didn't care a bit."

"That is a serious matter. I mean them offering you money. The harassment is worse. Let's start with the department you work in." Dupree pulled a legal pad from his desk drawer.

"I'm Leif Carlsson's secretary."

"The vice-president?"

"Yes, I was Josh Stanton's assistant until the sale. I need this job, so I stayed. Now I'm just a secretary."

"Is he the problem?"

"He is all over me. It started out just a touch on the arm when he would come to my desk. Then he kept going further, and further. Once he reached around from behind and squeezed my breast."

"What did you do?"

"I jumped up and screamed at him. Told him to never touch me again."

"How did he respond?"

"He laughed." Tomi's eyes were full of fire. "He said things too. Filthy things. What he would like to do to me. Remarks about my clothes and body. I hate him!"

"So that prompted you to go to HR?"

"He was standing at his door with a rep from California. He was telling the guy how he would like to bend me over the desk and…" She began to cry. "It was so degrading." She sobbed.

"That was today?"

Tomi nodded. "As soon as he closed his door I left."

Dupree cleared his throat. "Who did you see in HR?"

"The new director. Pilson? Pilmer?"

"Pilmend."

"Yes, her. She started out OK, but as I told her about what I had put up with she started to make excuses. 'I'm sure it is just a misunderstanding.' Can you imagine? She took out a checkbook. She wrote a check and pushed it across the desk with a form she pulled from a folder."

"Saying?"

"Saying, by accepting the check I agreed to keep quiet, basically. Hush money."

"How much was the check?"

"I don't know. I didn't look. I was so mad. I said something I probably shouldn't, then left. They can't do that, can they? I mean, aren't there laws?"

Dupree sat silently and pretended to write meaningful things on his note pad. He was too angry to speak. This girl, for that's what she appeared to be, was misused by the company. The more she spoke, the clearer he saw her. She was different than the women who came with similar complaints. They were mostly married or divorced, and more mature in the ways of the world. Tomi was shocked, embarrassed and wanted justice. There was a naiveté in her demeanor that projected an innocence that this crude assault on her emotions and person both shocked and terrified her.

Dupree was caught in an ethical trap. He wanted to go punch Carlsson's lights out. He wanted to demand to see the checkbook. He wanted justice for the poor young woman that sat across from him. But, he couldn't.

He was the one in the company that was paid to defend these guys. He was corporate counsel. Now that he heard her story though, she was covered by the attorney-client privilege. Likewise, he couldn't file suit against his employer. His head spun with a whirlwind of law, compassion, and anger. He was bound to not help her. He was morally appalled at her situation. He was conflicted beyond his emotional, and professional ability to think straight.

"So what can you do?" Tomi interrupted his scribbling and thoughts.

"I want you to go home. I'll make the excuse. Do not, I repeat, do not, tell anybody about our talk or your trip to HR. Clear? It is very important that they don't catch wind of this upstairs. I have no doubt Ms. Pilmend has already called Mr. Carlsson. We need you out of the building before he calls me. OK?"

"But,"

"But, nothing. Go."

Tomi picked her bag up from the floor next to the chair. "Tomorrow?"

"If you're ready, come in. Otherwise, call in sick." Dupree tried to smile reassuringly but his heart wasn't in it.

"Thank you." Tomi nodded softly.

"Not yet." Dupree stood. "This may get uglier before it gets better. I just want you to be aware."

"Yes sir, I understand."

I wonder if you do, Dupree thought.

Tomara French closed the door of her Honda Civic. She sat still for a long moment then crossed her arms on the top of the steering wheel, rested her head against them and sobbed. Ecomm was her first real job. She was twenty years old. Two years out of high school, Community College dropout, and never had a serious boyfriend.

Tomi was the oldest of five kids. She was homeschooled through eighth grade. High school was a dreamland of friends and caring teachers. New Hope Christian High School and its student body of fifty kids were like an extended family, a throwback to the days of no cell phones, no internet, school uniforms, and chapel. The only computers were in a Secretarial Skills class.

The girls outnumbered the boys three to one. Mark Wilson taught Boys P.E. and what it meant to be a gentleman. Any report of ungentlemanly conduct was met with laps around the track, or wind sprints, short dashes at full speed of about thirty yards, back and forth until the offender was winded. The lecture, a combination of the teacher's disappointment, disgust, and anger usually did the trick and there were few, if any, repeated offenses.

The girls of the school were taught directly from Proverbs. The Old Testament *description of The Wife of Noble Character was the guiding text for their training.*

It was certainly politically incorrect, and often held up to ridicule by the community, but the teaching was not some tenant of religious zealots, rather a return to the values that built the nation and were seen as values more practical than political. No one expected the girls to comply with the examples completely. Part of the graduation requirements at the tiny unaccredited High School was for every girl to memorize and recite the thirty-one verses. Tomi scored highest in her class, reciting the passage word for word perfect on her first attempt.

For the girls of New Hope, the concept of serving and cherishing her family was the point of the Proverbs curriculum. Most of the girls would and did, marry after graduation. In the small communities in and around White Owl, they started their families and raised children that rarely strayed from the teaching of their faith and the lessons their mother learned in her multi-denominational schooling.

Tomi chose a different path. She wanted more education so she enrolled at Edmonds Community College. She seemed to flourish in the large population of students in the rolling, wooded, eco-friendly campus. No doubt she would have graduated and even gone on to a four-year college, but the death of her father brought it all to an end.

Ecomm came to White Owl a month after her beloved father's sudden passing and she was first in line at the first Ecomm Job Faire. Her paperwork stood out for not only her certificates in typing and computer skills but for her elegant, print-like handwriting. It caught the attention of a graphics design coordinator as her resume was passed along the table of department representatives.

Tomi was taken directly to Joshua Stanton who oversaw the artistic and creative divisions of the company. Her quiet, yet confident, persona won Stanton over completely and she became his administrative assistant. He was delighted at her honesty when she suggested that perhaps she was unqualified for such a lofty position.

"Miss French, that is exactly why I want you for the job." Stanton smiled. "You are honest enough to tell me the truth, not what you think I want to hear. We'll train you as we go along. What do you say?" Stanton smiled reassuringly.

"I always tell the truth sir, thank you." Tomi got the job and was a perfect sounding board and advocate for her boss.

When the company was sold Stanton offered to introduce her to friends in big companies where he was sure she would be valued and well paid. She was so tempted to accept, but her mother and siblings depended on her income to supplement the small check from Social Security each month.

On the last day at the company, Joshua Stanton gave Tomi the keys to a deep blue Honda Civic. He said he picked the color because it matched her eyes. It was the only time he made any comment on her looks. His respect ran so deep for Tomi he never swore around her or let anyone else, without a hard look and a warning about 'language'.

Breaking all the unspoken barriers of protocol and office etiquette they followed, Joshua Stanton gave Tomi a hug and a gentle kiss on the cheek and he thanked her for her inspiration and loyalty as he said good-bye. Tomi blushed for ten minutes after. She knew she loved him, and he loved her.

"Melinda, got a second?" Dupree called from his desk.

"What's up?"

"This is going to sound really silly, but when you want to call in sick and you're not really sick, you just need a break, who do you call? What do you say?"

"Mr. Dupree! I would never!"

"Yeah, the lady doth protest too much, methinks." Dupree grinned and let her know she could speak freely.

"You can't beat the old, "time-of-the-month cramps thing". Usually, a call to Janet in HR at the clerical pool desk takes care of coverage."

"How close to Ms. Pilmend is she?"

"Nobody is close to her." Melinda sneered.

"I meant physically. If you call in, does Pilmend know?"

"No, that's a different office down the hall."

"Do me a favor. Call clerical and tell her you saw Tomi French throwing up and told her to go home. And Melinda, please keep it our little secret."

"No problem." Melinda looked at Dupree with a combination of mystery and admiration.

After Melinda returned to her desk. Dupree sat staring down at the yellow pad on his desk. His notes were a combination of doodles, underlined words and partial sentences, all of which screamed of his anger and frustration at the continued pattern of harassment and hostile work environment since the company changed hands.

He looked at his watch, almost ten. Dupree took the folder from the top of the stack awaiting his attention. His focus was just sharpening on the documents in front of him when his phone rang.

About the Author

Micheal Maxwell has traveled the globe on the lookout for strange sights, sounds, and people. His adventures have taken him from the Jungles of Ecuador and the Philippines to the top of the Eiffel Tower and the Golden Gate Bridge, and from the cave dwellings of Native Americans to The Kehlsteinhaus, Hitler's Eagles Nest! He's always looking for a story to tell and interesting people to meet.

Micheal Maxwell was taught the beauty and majesty of the English language by Bob Dylan, Robertson Davies, Charles Dickens, and Leonard Cohen.

Mr. Maxwell has dined with politicians, rock stars and beggars. He has rubbed shoulders with priests and murderers, surgeons and drug dealers, each one giving him a part of themselves that will live again in the pages of his books.

Micheal Maxwell has found a niche in the mystery, suspense, genre with The Cole Sage Series that gives readers an everyman hero, short on vices, long on compassion, and a sense of fair play, and the willingness to risk everything to right wrongs. The Cole Sage Series departs from the usual, heavily sexual, profanity-laced norm and gives readers character-driven stories, with twists, turns, and page-turning plot lines.

Micheal Maxwell writes from a life of love, music, film, and literature. Along with his lovely wife and travel partner, Janet, divide their time between a small town in the Sierra Nevada Mountains of California, and their lake home in Washington State.

Made in the USA
Columbia, SC
27 April 2021